Annabel

By

Anthony Macey

First published in Great Britain in 2012 via Lulu Publications by Anthony Macey

Paperback ISBN-978-1-4717-7766-0

E-Book ISBN-978-1-4717-7768-4

Cover Image by ©Nathan White

Cover Design by ©Anthony Macey

Foreword

The thank you list;

My daughter Isabel, for her regular sleeping patterns that gave me time to complete this.

Jacqui for being there at the very beginning and seeing it through to the very end. Apologies it took five years in between.

Amy and Paul for reading the very rough first draft with Jacqui and to all of you for all giving the exact same piece of feedback independently which helped me improve it a great deal.

Graeme for reading the redraft and being so positive and Nigel for doing the same and being my self appointed weapons specialist. Your insight was exceptionally useful and any errors that remain are purely down to artiistic licence on my part.

Kim for proof reading the final, final draft, great job and it means I can blame the remaining errors on you...

Iain for your exceptionally insightful words of wisdom towards the book cover and not just taking my money and doing it yourself.

Nathan for taking the cover photograph and agreeing to let me use it free of charge without any copyright lawsuits (I have the emails...).

The many authors; Stephen King, Shaun Hutson, Terry Brooks, David Gemmell, James Follett, Tom Clancy, Robin Hobb, Joe Dever, Haruki Murakami, Bret Easton Ellis, Margaret Weis and Tracy Hickman for the fantastic books of theirs I have read over the years and which helped to inspire me to write my own.

All the rest (and by no means least); All the many bands, musicians, composers and producers who made the music to keep me sane. Simon and Michael. Suky. Madelon. My English teacher Gillian, History Teacher Paul and Music Teacher Roland. Taz, Anita, Bronwen, Liz and the rest of my friends at "The Don". Uncle Les, Tammy, Kara, my wonderful Nan and of course Strawberry.

For anybody I missed I apologise profusely and will make it up to you in the sequel...

I hope you all enjoy the book.

Anthony

Prologue

"Jesus, what on earth are you doing out here in this weather?"

Shielding her eyes from the wind she looked up at the silhouette standing above. The gloomy light that the thick, overcast sky allowed entry to, left the figure mostly in shadow. The man, for the voice implied as much, was reasonably tall, wearing well tailored clothes and shoes but, maybe most importantly of all, there appeared to be genuine concern in his voice. Slowly. Deliberately. She pushed herself up. The pavement beneath, cold concrete, further chilling her already cold hands, red and sore from the exposure.

"I..." A sleek black car came to a halt at the foot of the curb, distracting the man's attention, interrupting her... her what? Explanation? What was to explain? The situation was obvious and the question therefore rhetorical. The man strode towards the car, his smooth, handsome face coming properly in to view for the first time. Her impressions of his clothes were apparently correct as they looked both well made and expensive, although everything looked expensive to her of late. He reached for the car and pulled open the door. She sank towards the floor again, so much for concern.

"Are you going to get in? Staying here would be a little silly do you not think?"

He was stood by the open door waiting for her response. She looked at him wearily, invites in to strangers cars, could be trouble but then again it was so cold. To stay here *would* be silly. More importantly, if it was anything like last night it would be bordering on *suicidal!* The man bent down and reached out a gloved hand, open, inviting, friendly. Once again she began to rise and with his help, worked her cold, cramped legs to a standing position. She could already feel the warmth of the cars heater and was suddenly eager to be close to it, unafraid and reckless to any obvious dangers posed by the situation. Regardless of the risks, she weighed that, should she be hurt or even killed, it would just be an unexpected turn of fate to arrive in this form instead of on the cold streets that had been her home.

She sat on the far side of the car and the man seated himself on the opposite side, fastening his seatbelt, gesturing that she should do the same. He leaned forwards and spoke softly to the driver. Who smiled and pulled away in to the traffic.

He turned to her, smiling but somehow sadness and pity were reflected in his eyes. No not pity, something else, protectiveness she could not quite explain. "My name is Sebastian, my old friend in the front there is Karl." The driver nodded slightly to her in his rear view mirror. They both looked at her expectantly. What? What did they want from her? The man looked at her and then softly, asked "And what is your name my dear?" She suddenly felt silly at the obviousness of it but it had been awhile since anybody had cared enough to actually ask.

"Annabel."

Chapter 1

The journey was completed in silence. The man, Sebastian, did not speak again. She felt she should ask something, like where on earth they were going but for some reason she felt she did not have the right and that to do so would be rude. She did not wish to be rude. She was feeling warm, properly warm, for the first time since summer. Feeling had returned to parts of her body she had forgotten existed, including her heart. She no longer felt emotionally isolated for some unexplainable reason and was becoming aware, unhappily so, of her attire and her appearance. The dress she wore was matted with grime and dirt, as was the jumper she was wearing over the top of it. Her tights were so badly worn and laddered she might as well have not been wearing any and her once pretty, red, heeled shoes were now scuffed and lack lustre. She could not see her face but knew she would look a mess, the inside of the car was so clean, and she would be making it dirty. An overwhelming need to apologise gripped her and felt ashamed for reasons she could not place. She looked up at the man who had welcomed her, dirty, torn, a mess, in to his shiny, clean car. "I... I'm sorry for... I'll be making the car... I'm so filthy!" She began to cry in despair, angry with herself for showing weakness, for being upset, for everything. She felt a warm touch to her hand. "If the dirt and grime bothers you so, then it is something we shall have to remedy is it not?" He released her hand and turned back to the window. His words comforting but somehow unexpected. She too turned her attention to monolithic buildings passing by outside the window, the few people walking through the cold, the wind ripping at them ferociously and rain beginning to fall. Whatever happened now she was thankful that for the time being at least, she had somehow been granted solace from the unrelenting weather outside. It was then that she began to ponder what the cost might be. As she turned to ask, the car came to a halt outside a tall apartment building, the entranceway gleamed with the light inside. She suddenly felt a pang of bitterness, the kind of place that would not offer people like her some shelter in weather like this, the kind of place people like her were not allowed within fifty feet of.

The man called Sebastian opened his door and stepped from the car. "Are you coming or do you intend to stay in the car?" He asked invitingly, kindly. She felt tears again beginning to build as she realised it had been a long, long time since anyone had spoken to her so tenderly. Her bitterness quickly diminished as she slid across the seat to the open door, grimacing as she saw the trail of dirt she had left behind. Almost as if reading her thoughts Karl turned and said "Do not trouble yourself Miss Annabel, I shall tend to it tonight." As Sebastian closed the door she caught a glimpse of Karl's smiling, kindly face and then he and the car were gone, lost in the river of traffic. Sebastian led her to the entrance and as the doorman held the glass door open for them she saw the slightest hint of disgust and scorn at the corners of his forced smile, betrayed by his eyes as they momentarily locked. She tried not to care, it was nothing she was not used to but now she did care, for some reason she felt that this man, Sebastian, would see the look in the doorman's eyes and he would suddenly realise the mistake he had made by bringing her here and then discard her, back in to the bitter cold outside.

He leaned close to her ear, this was it, he was going to tell her he had made a mistake...

"The doorman, Paul. I would not worry, he looks at everyone like that."

She knew it was a lie but was thankful for it anyway. The elevator doors stood open as if they were waiting for them and she followed Sebastian inside. Annabel stood uncomfortably to the side of the lift with her arms hugging her chest, her raggedy bag, all of her possessions contained within, clutched tightly in her hand. The elevator came to a halt and the doors opened on a short passageway to a door.

"This is us."

Sebastian stepped from the elevator and she followed. His hand moving the key swiftly to the lock in a fluid practiced motion, allowing it to swing open on it's well oiled hinges to reveal the room beyond. It was beautiful. Simple but beautiful none-the-less. The walls were painted in a subtle off-white colour, the furniture all in the same deeply contrasting black. The room she could see was the lounge area and she kicked off her shoes without realising as she stepped through the entrance. The edge of the room was about a foot higher than the centre of the room which was depressed and reached via elegant, hanging stairs, also in black. Behind this, the dining area was visible through an archway, a long black table, surrounded by high backed chairs. Everything looked so immaculate and once again she felt very out of place, a dark smudge on a white canvas, in more ways than one. Even Sebastian seemed to meld seamlessly with the decor and furniture.

"This way if you would."

He led her through a different archway she had not yet noticed and to one of the doors lining it. A gleaming white bathroom beyond, again, spotlessly clean. The chrome finish of the taps glimmering in the light.

"No gold plumbing?" She laughed hollowly, hoping the joke would help to fill the divide.

"No, I find gold tacky." He smiled kindly again. "I thought that maybe you would like to... powder your nose?"

She laughed. Her first proper laugh in as long as she could remember. Tonight appeared to be a night of firsts. "You sort yourself out here and I shall go and see if I can sort you out some temporary attire while we have your current garments cleaned, feel free to use whatever you wish."

She thought to say that burning them might be a better solution than cleaning but he was already gone, so she turned her attention to the extravagant and yet minimalist bathroom. It was the subtleties that were what made it extravagant. No gold but a large bubble jet bath, separate power shower, built in cupboards, exceptionally placed tiles. She turned on the water to the bath and found some bubble bath in a virtually seamless sliding cupboard beside it. She slowly undressed and laid her clothes in a pile on the floor, uncomfortably aware of the dirty marks her feet were leaving on the white tiles. Stepping down in to the bath she felt luxury, paradise, warmth. Tonight was, so far, unquestionably the best night of her life. The warmth of the water, the soothing aroma of the foam, she could almost feel the life preceding this moment seeping from her pores, cleansed away by the water. A knock on the door brought her attention back to the present and Sebastian entered carrying a white robe and some towels. Annabel sank lower in to the water, uncomfortable that only the foam was hiding her exposed body.

"Apologies, you will have to trust that I am not looking." To her surprise and, more surprisingly, her dismay, he kept to his word and his eyes did not stray from the task at hand. He left closing the door behind him as he did. She lay in the water, the jets softly massaging her skin. As clichéd as it felt thinking it, this was like a dream she kept waiting to wake up from. Less than a few hours ago she was lying, shivering, on a dilapidated cardboard sheet, with the elements draining her life away and now... Now she was having a hot bath, relaxing, inside, in the warm. *At what cost?* The thought returned to haunt her. Why would he be doing this? What would he want in return? She pushed the uncomfortable thoughts from her mind and after enjoying the warm, massaging water a little longer, emerged from the bath and released the water. She looked at her naked body in the full length mirror that surrounded the sink. The occasional bruise mottled her skin as did a network of tiny scratches, mainly on her legs. What shocked her most was her gaunt appearance. Since she had left she had lost far too much weight than was healthy. Her hair looked a lot better now she had washed it properly but it was not as nice as it once was, long blonde and flowing. Her stunning green eyes had aged a thousand years too, although her face still remained by all accounts youthful and fresh. The naturally fine hair on her legs appeared coarse and obvious to her eyes as did the tufts below her arms and between her legs. Scrabbling in one of the cupboards she found a razor and carefully sought to improve these areas, frustrated at how alien the implement now felt in her hands as she tried to remedy what she saw as a manageable blemish on her appearance. Bending to the rack she picked up one of the towels, finding the rack had heated them and felt as good as the water had against her freshly washed skin. Wrapping the towel around her hair, she slipped in to the comfortable robe Sebastian had provided and slipped on some slippers he had also supplied, opened the door and wandered outside to find him.

Sebastian was not in the lounge area so she walked through to the dining area and then smelt... heaven. Walking along the length of the dining area, admiring the view through the hanging blinds as she did, Annabel strode through an opening in to a spacious kitchen. It was in the same style as the rest of what she had seen of the apartment, the exception being, this was not so tidy. Pots and pans sat on the hob and something cooked in the oven. Sebastian was cooking something in a wok over a separate gas hob and, as she entered, red flames jumped from the pan and Sebastian turned to smile at her. "The food shall be finished shortly, so if you would like to make yourself at home until then." Following which he returned his attention to the food cooking around him.

Annabel considered exploring the rest of the apartment but instead decided to sit and wait at the dining table, noticing that two places had been set with cutlery and plates. After a short time Sebastian appeared laden with plates and bowls of food. He laid them on the table before disappearing back in to the kitchen. Annabel's stomach immediately began to ache and her mouth to water. The food smelt and looked wonderful. Unable to stop herself she reached to the closest plate and began eating, gorging herself on whatever she could reach, only stopping as Sebastian entered with more food. Immediately the shame returned but again his smile calmed her. "Please, continue. I expect it has been a while since you were last able to eat so well." Smiling gratefully, Annabel resumed eating, albeit in a more civilised manner. Taking a mixture of food from the virtual banquet that Sebastian had supplied. Sweet potatoes, creamed potatoes, carrots, peas, corn, salad, pasta, ham, beef, chicken, the choices appeared endless. As the plates quickly emptied and she had her fill, she began to feel a slight pang of indigestion from where she had eaten too fast and, probably too much, in the beginning. So when Sebastian inquired "Dessert?" she woefully declined with a shake of her head, not particularly wishing to be sick.

"So Annabel, may I call you Annabel?"

"Annabel will be fine, thank you."

He stood and walked around the table to where she had sat and reached towards her. She recoiled slightly as he did, realising now what it was he wanted in return for his "kindness". She looked away but reached up to pull the robe open. He stopped her. "No. That is not what I was doing." He continued to reach and pulled up the sleeves of the robe, twisting her arms around and inspecting them. Satisfied he let her arms go and smiled again. "Do you do drugs?" Annabel realised she had been holding her breath and let it out as a sigh of relief and maybe some slight disappointment.

"No. No drugs."

"Drink?"

"I'm not an alcoholic if that's what you mean. I used to drink occasionally before I... before. Not now though as it was more important to eat."

"Sell your body?"

"Excuse me?"

"Did you ever prostitute yourself?" His manner had remained unchanged and his tone was still kindly but that did not make it feel like any less of an interrogation.

"No. Never."

"I apologise if those questions were personal but I needed to know to what extent I would be helping you."

Shrugging she nodded. If he was going to have somebody in his home then he had every right to know if they were a junkie, or get drunk and mug him as soon as his back was turned. "It's okay. What do you mean by helping me?"

"All in good time. Criminal record?"

"No."

"Would that be because you have never committed a crime or because you have never been caught?"

She paused, looking up at him. "Sometimes, when you're out there, you do what you have too. I need to eat. I need to stay warm. I..." He cut her off.

"Of course. You need not justify yourself to me. A crime of necessity, of survival, is not the same as a crime of greed."

"Thank you."

"For?"

"For understanding. For the bath? For dinner? For taking me out of the cold? For everything!" She realised how indebted she was to this man already, having only known him a short time. As grateful as she was for his help the growing debt was making her uncomfortable. "Why are you helping me?"

"Why not?"

"Do you make a habit of picking up young girls off the street then?"

He raised an eyebrow. "Do you think that is likely?"

"I guess not."

Sebastian looked in to her eyes and then stared off out of the window, deep in thought. "I am very fortunate Annabel. I was born of money and have never had to want for anything. I am strong, intelligent, successful. Anything I desire is available to me on a whim." He turned back to her. "Seeing you sat on the side of the road in that terrible weather struck a chord with me. The stark contrasts to our lives I have to admit ignited a curiosity in me. That somebody should find themselves in such a situation as you do, nowhere to live, without ability to eat, no facility to clothe yourself properly. It not only pains me, it intrigues me. Do you understand?" Annabel nodded silently, the feeling of relief that he had decided to help her spreading warmly through her stomach. She began to realise how fortunate she had been. Right place, right time. "One last thing Annabel."

"Yes?"

He took her hands in his own and looked deeply in to her eyes. "I wish for you to tell me your story, all of it. No gaps, secrets or lies." A pause followed. It stretched for what appeared to be hours. Their eyes remain locked, it seemed such a simple request, meaningless almost but she had a lot to tell. To tell it *all*? She had never told anyone all of it. She could lie of course but he had specifically requested that she did not. She continued to mull it over and he continued to hold her hands and look in to her eyes.

Finally she turned her head to the side, gazing through the slits in the blind and pulled her hands away. It appeared this was indeed going to be a night of many firsts.

Chapter 2

Steph wiped the blood from his face.

"You okay mate?"

Alex looked over at him from a few feet away. They were both lying on their stomachs in DPM, virtually invisible among the dense undergrowth of the forest floor.

"Yeah. Fucking thorn whipped my face. That's all."

"This op is fuckin' born. Getting us out on our tods in this bloody weather. Crawling around like a bloody snake when we should be having a piss up to keep warm!"

"Teamwork and all that eh?"

They stopped talking as an 'enemy' patrol came within a few feet of their location. The black boots so close at one point Stephen Thebe could smell the sweet scent of the fresh polish on them. As the patrol disappeared, Steph signalled to Alex. "Come on, let's get this bullshit over with." They scrambled forwards until they were overlooking the base camp and waited. Two minutes later a flare went up and Steph sprang forward with Alex following behind. Jumping out on the four man patrol that had passed them earlier they let off two quick shots each.

"Bang. You're dead you wanker."

"Yeah, yeah. Fuck off Steph."

Laughing good naturedly at Higgsy and the rest of their patrol they left them behind as they advanced on the target.

"Macca and Doug should be out with the hostage any second, I'll take position up there you take a flanking position on that ridge to offer covering fire as planned."

"Righty-ho."

"Oh and Alex."

"Yeah?"

"Try not to get shot you wanker."

"Fuck off." Laughing in low voices they split up and went to their positions. A few minutes later the door burst open and two men in camouflage emerged with a man in civvies between them. As they headed across the clearing backing the cabin shots rang out sending them to ground. Fire rang out from somewhere on the ridge where Alex was in position and some cursing sounded from a clump of bushes. Chuckling to himself Steph sent another volley in that direction as figures began appearing from behind it.

"OI YOU CUNTS! WE'RE ALREADY FUCKING DEAD!!"

In reply Doug stood too and released a carefully aimed shot at the leader of the group. Laughing uncontrollably as the patrol dived for cover they all, eventually, converged to the centre of the clearing as a horn sounded the end of the exercise.

"Okay lads settle down."

"We're settled Sir. But Anderson's group are a little sour so are licking their wounds."

"Thank you Macca..."

"Better than licking their balls eh lads?"

"Yes Doug. THANK YOU!" Together they walked back towards base camp, the banter and laughter continuing.

"Teambuilding exercises eh? What a fucking waste of time."

"Fun though Alex." Steph winked and nodded at Matthew Higgs rubbing a red welt appearing on his neck.

They all headed to the showers and cleaned themselves up, cleaning off the dirt that had accumulated crawling through the mud. As Steph returned to his bag Higgsy walked past to the sound of further jeers from Steph and his team mates.

"Yeah, okay Steph you've had your laugh now."

"Yeah because we won."

"Bastard."

Grinning widely he stood next to him getting dressed. "Hey up mate who's this fit little filly?" He reached in to Steph's bag and pulled out a photograph of an attractive young blonde girl. Steph's attitude immediately changed. "Give it back... now."

"Ooh look, Steph is getting all worked up because I've found a picture of his latest girlfriend."

"I'm not playing Higgs. Give me it back." His voice was low. Dangerous. Angry. But Higgsy was too caught up in the moment to notice.

"Hey no need to be so uptight Steph. I just wanted to know if I can have a go on the little tart once you're done."

Steph swung at Higgsy and connected solidly with his jaw. A loud crack sounded and Higgsy slumped straight to the floor, photograph still held in his hand. Steph stepped over him, bent down and picked up the picture, his mind in a world apart from everyone around him. His attention slowly returned to the present as he tore his eyes from the picture and noticed that 3 of the guys were helping Higgsy to his feet.

"Fucking hell Steph what was that about?"

"I warned him Alex. I don't mind a joke but not about my sister."

He stuffed the rest of his belongings in to his bag, grabbed it up, turned on his heel and left without another word.

Chapter 3

Pushing the button on the dashboard lifted the door to the garage, allowing Karl to park without having to brave the ferocious rain that was now hammering from the sky. The sound of it hitting the roof of the Bentley Continental GT was enough to convince anyone inside that it was being covered with pocks and dents and, this, this was a car designed to keep the noise outside, just that. Outside. Turning the engine off Karl opened the door and stepped out in to the spacious workshop as the strip light overhead settled after being activated automatically upon his exit from the car. Stainless steel shutters lined the walls which housed, amongst other things, the extensive collection of tools he used in order to maintain the car. *Not that cars these days need much maintenance*, he thought sentimentally. Since the change to the Bentley, there was hardly anything he could touch on it. Mostly they were controlled and monitored by a central computer. *It is lovely to drive though.* He made to the door at the exterior and entered his key code to unlock it, the door sliding aside to reveal a personal lift up to the main house. The small lift carried Karl upwards quickly, his image dully reflected in the doors. He suddenly realised how much he had aged, no longer was the youthful man of *ten no... Twenty years ago? Had it been so long?* Of course he had not been working for Sebastian then, he would barely have been a child but still the rate at which time passed was impressive, intimidating even. He looked at the once dark hair, now with shocks of steely grey becoming ever more commonplace. The once smooth face was becoming careworn and even though he had shaved that morning, the so called 'five o'clock shadow' was more than a little pronounced for the time that had passed. Karl was still very much healthy though and felt a glimmer of pride about his strong, muscular form. Broad shoulders, hard stomach and thick arms, almost missable under the subtle guise of his clothes. Looking in to his own grey eyes, the doors opened, removing the image before him. Exiting on to a long passageway decorated very differently to the apartment building he had just left, he stopped momentarily to turn on the lights from a panel, discreetly enclosed behind a painting, then once again continued down the passage, stopping at a locked door three quarters of the way down. Removing a key card, he entered it in to a small crack in the wall concealed by the frame and simultaneously looked in to the keyhole where a laser read, and confirmed the veracity of both. The door clicked in confirmation, swinging open to reveal the room beyond. The room was spacious and tidy, much more contemporary and minimalist than the rest of the house, it was obvious that the same direction was being attempted here as at the apartment. An entire wall on the left-hand side was occupied by a screen, stretching the length and breadth of it. On the opposite side of the room a translucent desk was placed with several flat screen monitors organised and suspended at its edge. The wall immediately opposite as you entered was sheer and plain, only upon closer inspection were the extremely subtle seams of small sliding panels apparent. The ceiling was mirrored in its entirety. Only the room below could be seen in its sharp reflection but even the most naive of people would instinctively know that it was where they were being watched from.

"Call office."

The wall with the screen immediately flared in to life, segregating itself in to a space in the centre reading 'Connecting... Office' and a smaller, separate square showing an image of Karl. The space in the centre changed from 'Connecting' to 'Connected' and sat frozen waiting for instructions.

"Open communication." The square now became the face of a middle aged man. *Useless idiot of a man. Sebastian should have removed him ages ago.* For some reason though Sebastian had seen fit *not* to remove him and he was therefore now on the screen in front of Karl, his moronic glaze apparent even under the face of impassion he was trying to convey. "Sebastian wished for me to notify the office that he would be unavailable until 10.00am tomorrow morning, any situation requiring immediate action or attention on his behalf, should first be viewed by myself in order to establish the importance before he is unnecessarily inconvenienced."

"As Sebastian wishes, Mr Rotschlossen." He nodded curtly and Karl severed the connection with a wave of his hand. He left the room, using the same process as he had when he entered, and proceeded around a corner and down another passageway in the direction of his room, upon reaching the entrance to which he hurriedly stepped inside. It had been a long day and if there were any problems it could be a long night too. Without bothering to shower or undress, he collapsed on to the bed staring up at the ceiling. His thoughts wondered to the homeless girl Sebastian had 'rescued' from the side of the road. The extent that Sebastian's compassion could, indeed *would*, stretch too, often amazed him. To think that he would take that dirty, foul smelling girl, not only in to his car but also in to his private apartment in order to protect her from the elements bemused Karl somewhat, especially as it was so common a sight these days, the homeless, scrounging on the streets. What had provoked Sebastian to save this one, at this time was something only Sebastian knew. *Or perhaps even he does not know why he did it?* Bored with asking himself unanswerable questions, Karl closed his eyes and turned his thoughts to sleep. Sleep is where they remained until the mobile phone he had placed on his bedside began to ring.

Chapter 4

It had started to rain, the weather mirroring Annabel's face as tears had begun to glide softly from the corner of her eyes and down her cheeks. She had deliberately not thought about her life. The need to survive, the cold and pain of living on the streets had been enough to numb the memory but now, in the warm safety of this kind man's apartment, words and protection, there was nothing to numb the memory, or to numb the pain the memories brought with them. She spoke abruptly.

"I was six." She looked over at Sebastian and he looked back impassively, waiting patiently, listening. Realising he was going to say nothing, merely wait for her to finish, without interruption, she continued. "My dad, my real dad. He died." Her eyes were beginning to sting now and she had not even begun. "It was some form of cancer I think, I don't really know, my mum never really spoke about it with me and I was too young to really know what was going on. I remember him being in the hospital for a long time, tubes coming out of his mouth and nose. Drips in his arm, machines beeping. Then one day, he was just dead. My mum was upset, well I thought she was but my dad had some sort of insurance through work so we got a lot of money which meant that we were okay financially. My mum stopped talking to me after that and I kind of went inside myself. I felt really alone as other than my mum I didn't have any family and she wouldn't talk to me anymore. I had virtually no friends and those I did have didn't understand, they were 6, why would they?" She went on. "It was like that for two or three years, mum became more and more distant, while I started to fend for myself more and more. I would make my own meals, wash my clothes. She didn't mistreat me. She just didn't take the time to think I might have been feeling as bad as she was. Then, a few weeks after my ninth birthday, she changed. She became happier again, would walk around the house singing to herself. She still didn't talk to me much or spend any time with me but she would smile at me when we passed each other. It was a few weeks later that I discovered what, or rather who, was responsible for the change." She paused before continuing. "Rory." She said the word with distaste, pain apparent on her face as she did so and fresh tears began streaming from her eyes. "I never found out how they met, don't suppose it matters much, but he was the difference. To begin with I was glad, I thought mum was finally getting over dad and living her life again, I hoped we could be close again but I was wasting my time on hopes that weren't going to happen. A week after I met him Rory moved in, it was about a fortnight after that when it happened for the first time." She saw the look of sorrow behind his eyes as she said it and realised she had not been clear and he had misunderstood. She laughed hollowly. "Oh no, not that. I'm ashamed to say that I sometimes used to wish it *was* that but no. He came back to the house one night with mum. They had been out drinking and were both a mess. Mum fell over in the hallway and knocked some stuff over, waking me up, so I came down to see if everything was okay. When I got to the bottom of the stairs I could see that her eyes were closed and Rory was laughing."

"Your mum's a bit pissed me girl. She's gone and passed out in the hall." He was talking loudly, almost shouting at her.

"Is mum going to be okay?"

"Of course she will you bloody idiot, she's just drank too much that's all. Now fuck off back to bed." She looked up at him, frightened by his harsh words, no-one had ever spoken to her like that before, or used that kind of language in front of her, not deliberately at least and certainly not directed at her but her mother laying on the floor was more important to her than the drunken threat this man appeared to provide. She walked forwards and bent down to her mother's still form. She was breathing and stank of alcohol. She would be okay she supposed.

"I SAID BED YOU LITTLE FUCKER!" With that he struck her across the face, sending her frail form crashing back against the stairs. She lay there in pain and shock for several seconds before starting to cry. He bore down on her. "Don't start with that nonsense, or else." His voice was low and threatening, his breath thick with alcohol. He grabbed her wrist tightly and she felt fresh pain, then he proceeded to drag her up the stairs towards her room. She whimpered softly but was afraid to cry out in case he hit her again. When they reached the open door to her bedroom he threw her inside like a rag doll, her side crashing against her bed, adding to the increasing pain. He strode across the room towards her again. Long, powerful, intimidating strides that made her shrivel in to a ball. Then, as he stepped forwards, he brought his rear foot towards her stomach, hard, the pain causing her to double over in agony on the floor curling in to a ball. "Ugly little fucking leech. No wonder your mum was such a mess when she met me with a snot nosed little shit like you holding her back. I'm surprised she can live with herself giving birth to something as disgusting as you. You make me want to throw up." He spat in her face and left the room, leaving the tired, battered body of a thin nine year old girl lying beaten on the floor.

Annabel swallowed, strengthening her resolve. "I was lucky that time, it was only cuts and bruises. I told mum of course but she didn't want to hear it, didn't want to believe it. I don't think she could, not after he had been so nice to her. So I convinced myself that it had only happened because he was drunk, if mum loved him so much he couldn't be a bad person, but I was wrong, he could be a bad person. Was a bad person. It continued like that for several months, a year. They would get drunk and then he would beat the living shit out of me. I would pretend to be asleep so he wouldn't hurt me but he would beat me anyway, always telling me how ugly and disgusting I was. It became a way of life. I would try and avoid being at home and more importantly, avoid Rory and his beatings. They became steadily more and more frequent, whether he was sober or not. I started to get really disruptive at school until I got expelled when I was 12. Rory had my punishment all ready for me when I got home. I wondered why mum never stopped him, she must have known even though he never hit me in front of her, never called me those things he did while she could hear. I stopped being disruptive at school, I was getting too badly beaten at home because of it. I had no self esteem, no plans. I was just another troubled kid to everyone I guess. I lost my virginity when I was 13. He was 15 and he seemed nice enough. He didn't call me ugly or beat me, he said I was pretty. I think mostly he just said it to get in my pants but I lapped it up anyway." She gave a wry smile. "So I continued to get hit and insulted, so I slept with any guys who would have me, to make myself feel better. I started to get a reputation at school even though there had only been a few, I was still young, and eventually my parents found out from a guy who I wouldn't sleep with. I don't think he meant anything by it, he was just hurt because I said no, I think his mates ribbed him about it. If he had known how much trouble it caused me he wouldn't have done it. I remember smelling the alcohol as soon as I opened the front door. It was the day of my fifteenth birthday."

The smell was overpowering, there had been a lot of drinking going on she knew. She felt the familiar anxiety running down her spine as she tried to quietly close the door. The latch clicked and she heard movement from the lounge. Rory stood in the doorway leering at her with malice in his eyes. The soft sounds of her mother weeping in the background.

"In here. Now!" His voice was level but firm. There was a trace of something else there too, expectation? Satisfaction? As she entered she saw the empty bottle of Vodka clutched in her mother's hands and the redness of eyes caused by the tears. She stood and stumbled, so drunk she could barely stand. Annabel rushed forwards to steady her, holding her shoulder in support and then she noticed the disappointment and anger in her mother's eyes.

"You little slut." The words were icy, edged with acid, cutting deep. They hurt far more than the slap that followed the words, so much more that to begin with Annabel failed to realise her mother had even hit her. She looked in to her eyes questioningly. "I know about you! You sleeping around, you filthy little tramp!" The look in her mother's eyes brought tears to her own and she saw Rory smirking like a satisfied cat in the mirror behind her. Her mother collapsed back in to the chair, her eyes half closed, muttering drunken ramblings. She turned to leave the room but Rory blocked her exit.

"Not so fast, not so fast. It appears even an ugly little shit like you can get fucked if they offer it to enough people." He shoved past towards her mother. "Some people have no standards." He spun and hit her hard in the face sending her wheeling in to the door, sliding down it to collapse sitting on the floor. "I would rather fuck a dog myself." He sneered at her as she sat dazed. "You're not a patch on your mum. Now get out you ugly fucking pig." She scrambled out the door, leaning against the wall sobbing gently as she heard her *mum and him* begin to groan. She crawled away, stumbling as fast as she could up the stairs, away from it all, to the sanctity of her room. For a moment she wished that *he* liked *her* like he did her mother. *Perhaps he wouldn't treat me so badly then?*

"May I have a glass of water please?" Her sudden request was very out of place in the atmosphere the story had created but her throat was dry and she felt a need to continue. Unfazed Sebastian merely nodded, stood and took the empty jug from the table, returning a short while later with it full of chilled water and a freshly chilled glass. Annabel took a few sips and placed the glass on the table.

"I suppose you think I'm pretty messed up don't you? Wishing he wanted me?" She looked forcibly at him but his eyes remained calm and impassive. There was no sign of disgust there, or even pity. Only understanding. "Well, I don't suppose it matters much what you think. I think it's messed up." She wiped at her face. "Ten months later I discovered I was pregnant. It was with a guy I had been seeing for about six months. Stupidly I left the test in the bathroom. Rory found it and threw me down the stairs. I miscarried and almost died. It was then that I made the decision to runaway before he did the job properly."

Chapter 5

He knocked firmly on the door.

"Come in." The gravelly voice sounded through the thick oak, Steph twisted the handle and entered MacLeavey's office. The sun was glaring through the blinds lining the left hand side of the room, even though they were twisted to block as much out as possible. MacLeavey sat in his old leather chair behind the ancient, but imposing, mahogany desk he was working on. Behind him were some filing cabinets, mostly unused as everything was on computer these days. An up to date map of the world was clearly visible on the right hand side of the room but was by no means 'ordinary'. It was a TFT screen that updated in real time the ever changing borders of the world as the company became aware of them, which of course, was often far sooner than most governments. "Ah Stephen, thought it would be you, take a seat, please." Steph sat down in one of the leather chairs in front of the desk and made himself comfortable. *Thought it would be me? You knew as soon as I stepped within 200ft of the place you cheeky sod.* He smirked and MacLeavey smiled knowingly. MacLeavey had the air of a man who had been there. Where exactly, was the mystery, but there was no doubt as soon as you spent time with MacLeavey that he had been there anyway. Distinguished, witty, almost fatherly, you would be mistaken for thinking him to be harmless but even fathers can be dangerous given the correct circumstances.

"So Stephen." He sat with his old callused fingers interlaced in front of him, his elbows resting on the table. He peered out from under his bushy eyebrows, which matched his lion's mane of hair, with kindly eyes and smiled. Time passed. Steph shifted uncomfortably in his seat.

"So... what?"

MacLeavey continued to smile.

"Higgsy?"

The same look.

"Higgsy." He looked down at the table. "I'm sorry about that Sir but...
"

"No excuses Stephen. You went on a teambuilding exercise with
Matthew and proceeded to break his jaw." Steph sank a little lower in his
chair.

"But Sir..."

"AND!" He cut through Steph's retorts bringing silence back to the
room before continuing. "I hear that your team not only won outnumbered but
also successfully rescued the hostage." Steph looked up from the table and saw
the smile playing at the corners of MacLeavey's lips. "You and your team did
a sterling job. Of course Stephen this is marred somewhat by your inability to
suppress your anger concerning your sister." Taken aback at MacLeavey's
knowledge of this he started.

"Who said? One of the... "

"No. Not one of the others. You should know by now Stephen that
when you work for the Company we make it our business to know." Steph
pondered this a moment and realised that not only was it feasible it was pretty
obvious really. The company did not like surprises unless they were the ones
providing them. He had a sudden thought.

"Does the company *know* where my sister is?"

"No Stephen, unfortunately not. When you became officially
employed with us two years ago we were unable to find a trace of her after a
certain point." MacLeavey leaned closer. "Have you considered the possibility
that she may be dead?" Steph's face became fixed and hard. Yes he had
considered it, of course he had, but that did not mean it was so. Reading his
face MacLeavey continued. "Stephen. If the company are unable to locate her
with our resources then you will have to wait for her to find you." Steph
sighed, he knew it made sense but then, when did that ever change the way
anyone felt? "Now that is out of the way you can go and find Matthew. He's

refusing to work with you as he believes you will kill him the first chance you get. I told him of course this was nonsense as the first chance you had was in the showers, but for some reason this failed to console him." They both chuckled.

"I'll talk to him."

"Good because you're both working together soon, so be sure to resolve things sooner rather than later."

--

"Higgsy!" Steph shouted across the courtyard and increased to a trot. He saw Higgsy stop and turn his body in to a defensive stance. Steph chuckled to himself, he felt a little guilty but Higgsy's paranoia was both amusing and slightly flattering. He drew up a few feet from him and grinned widely. "Hello mate, how's the jaw?" Higgsy's *jaw* dropped open but as it had no strapping or pins and the action appeared to cause him no pain, Steph assumed MacLeavey had been exaggerating ever so slightly.

"MATE?!? JAW?!? YOU FUCKING...!" Steph hung his head slightly in apology.

"Look, Matt. About what happened. I'm sorry but it's a very touchy subject with me. I shouldn't have lost it with you but... I'm sorry."

"Well you fucking should be you cunt!" Higgsy dropped his defence very slightly and rubbed his jaw. "Luckily for you I don't hold grudges, so I'll let you buy me a drink to make up for it." The tension between them immediately dropped.

"I'm glad you didn't hold on to it mate. It was shit of me to hit you, it's just personal stuff you know?"

"Yeah, Alex explained it to me, well not all of it, not his place you know but I'm sorry for what I said. I just didn't know. When I found out I thought you were going to find me and finish the job!" He laughed humourlessly, glancing sideways to read Steph's face but he was placid and smiled back. "Pub then?"

"Sounds like a plan." They started jogging in the direction of the pub, located five miles down the road.

"I don't mean to pry mate but don't the company know where she is?"

"No mate, when MacLeavey pulled me in about our little tussle he told me as much." They both nodded to the guard in the security box as they headed through the perimeter. Higgsy turned to Steph, noticeably lowering his voice.

"You think he was telling the truth?"

Steph nodded, "They would have no reason to lie. If they knew where she was then telling me would help them. I'd be indebted to them for life, holding it from me wouldn't help."

They continued jogging, the lights of the pub now visible in the distance through the trees. "I guess so mate." But his voice lacked conviction.

Chapter 6

"Do you think you can find her then?" James Stock looked through the golden liquid in his glass, watching as it distorted the room, or maybe it was the quantity he had swallowed that had distorted the room. Mitchell Hale scratched his face as he pondered the question. "As I told you 12 months ago, I was unable to find any trace of her after April last year, it's like that with the homeless. They have no fixed address, few friends, nothing to trace. If this photograph is real then there may be a chance, no don't argue. I know what it *looks* like but you say you were sold this photograph, you have to be prepared to realise that this may have been altered. Also tracking down the car although not impossible, will be tricky. Even something as rare as that. Could have been a visitor to the area, anyone. If it was a local then we may stand a chance." The photograph he was referring too was a high resolution black and white snap of a young girl talking to a man in a car. The young girl appeared to be Christine Stock, James' daughter, the man in the car was unknown to him but hopefully he would have information concerning the girl. *Then again maybe not. She could have just been asking for directions or money. A coincidence. Of course there was always a chance...*

"So when will you start investigating again?" James broke in to his pondering, his voice slurred. *Poor bloke.* Mitchell knew that James blamed himself for the loss of his daughter, she had runaway after they had an argument about her being in trouble all the time, hanging out with the 'wrong crowd'. She upped and left, only sixteen. Legally she was allowed to leave home as long as she was safe. The police had been little help, having dealt with Christine personally a number of times, it came as no surprise to them when she disappeared. Some children could not be helped no matter how well meaning the parents. James was one of these parents.

"I'll start immediately for you James." He had a different case to finish but it was trivial. A wife wanting to know if her husband was cheating on her. If she was doubtful enough that she actually hired him, chances were he was, just a matter of collecting the photographs and that could be completed tonight. He would set off tonight. The landmark in the background, although distorted, gave a clear indication of the city, unfortunately the street could be any of a thousand there. Tracking the man would be the crucial part and to do that he would have to find the car, a sleek black Mercedes, not standard which would help finding it, as would the rarity of the model. "Do me a favour though."

"Favour?" James looked blearily at him, trying to focus.

"Try not to raise your hopes too much, it might turn out to be a dead end." James nodded sluggishly. "One more thing James." He reached forwards, taking James' glass and draining the contents. "Lay off the drink. If I do find her, she's not going to want to come home to a drunk." He smiled at James and patted his shoulder. James nodded, tears in his eyes. Mitchell always made a point of not getting emotionally involved with his clients. It just was not good business and made his job harder. With James though he had found it impossible, the emotional deterioration he had seen in the man had been very hard to bear, making his investigations all the more frustrating. The first time he had met James, the man had expected him to bring his daughter too him within a few days, after months of investigation he had hit a solid dead end. This photograph apparently came from around the time *of* that dead end. This left an uneasy feeling in his stomach. On top of which, being emotionally involved also made it harder to charge for his services. He had no choice of course, he had to eat, pay bills, pay expenses, but it did not make it any easier, especially when he was so involved with this case now. Mitchell rubbed his temples to relieve the stress, then stood to say his farewells.

"I'll contact you as soon as I have any information. Is this the only copy of the photograph?" James nodded. "Then I'll make some copies. Take care James, I'll talk to you soon." He smiled amicably and left the room. He looked at the photograph again. *Who took this and more importantly, why?* He knew it must have been something to do with the man in the car, the question was, what?

His thoughts lingered on this awhile longer as he exited the building, quickly running for his car and getting inside for the warmth. *First things first though, better see if I can get those pictures.* She would pay him tonight if he completed the job and it would give him some extra money for his trip. *Better to finish it now than pick things up when I get back.*

Chapter 7

Karl sprang awake immediately. He was one of those fortunate people that were immediately awake and alert, not requiring the normal post sleep recovery period to gather his senses. He reached over and answered the phone. "What is it?"

"Apologies for the disturbance at this hour Mr Rotschlossen but something set off a red flag so we. *I*, thought you would like to know immediately."

Karl's mind ran through the possibilities. A red flag could be set off for any number of trivial reasons but they were in place for a reason so it was good that they had not procrastinated in alerting him. "What was the cause of the flag?"

"Well Sir... it's a strange one, a little vague." Karl realised who it was he was talking to, Baxter. A very competent employee who was to oversee the finer details of things most would miss, he suddenly felt uneasy but was unsure why. "There was a DSE on Sebastian's former vehicle model."

A data search enquiry for a model of car that was no longer in their possession? What was Baxter playing at? "You woke me up for *this* Baxter? I thought more highly of you than that." He heard a nervous cough in reply from Baxter.

"Sir, with all due respect. The search, although general, was limited to within ten miles of a specified area, an area which encompasses both of Sebastian's local properties. This of course set off the automatic flag so I enquired further. The source who was searching for this information was also enquiring about specific upgrades to the vehicle, upgrades that were performed on Sebastian's vehicle while it was in his possession."

Karl thought on this. *Coincidence?* Maybe, but coincidences and a lot of trouble quite often came hand in hand so he was going to avoid taking any chances. "Okay Baxter, good work. I'm half a mind about whether to follow this up tonight or to leave it until tomorrow but I think for the moment it can wait. Unless... there's anything else you wish to inform me of?" There followed an uneasy silence on the other end of the phone, Karl could sense Baxter weighing up whether it was important enough to tell him. *Or maybe too important for him to know?* "Well...?"

Baxter coughed and cleared his throat. "There was one other thing Sir. A name, it was cross referenced along with the positive information results of the initial search."

"A name? Whose name? Somebody we know?"

"It is not a name that I am familiar with Sir, no."

"What is the name then Baxter, do not keep me in suspense all night!"

"Christine Stock." Baxter could hear nothing from the other end of the phone, a long silence followed and he shifted uncomfortably in his chair. "Sir, are you still there?" When the reply came the voice was devoid of any emotion.

"Yes. I am still here. I'll meet you at my office in forty-five minutes."

The phone clicked and went dead. Andrew Baxter sat in his office looking at the information on his computer screen and wished he had not let curiosity get the better of him. Christine Stock: Missing, Presumed Dead. He pulled on his jacket and fetched some water from the cooler. The information he had found stated that Christine Stock was last known to be living rough, having run away from home but searches for her had proved fruitless. Sebastian did not seem like the kind of man to pick up random homeless people, let alone the kind that would make their missing status more permanent. Of course what did he really know, the company that Sebastian ran most certainly had some suspect clientele. Okay maybe not suspect but very clandestine nonetheless. *Sebastian though? He's such a good man.* Sebastian was well known to his employees for his generosity and kindness. People were very rarely, if ever fired. If he thought the reason they should be fired was a result of unfortunate circumstance then they were allowed to stay, there was a lot of trust, all of it mutual. Baxter paced his office a little longer before he reached the decision that Sebastian was not the kind of person who would be involved in something as sinister as this appeared. To be fair to him, he was not certain there was even anything to be sinister, just a couple of coincidences that appeared to be linked. *Then why are you feeling like this?* It was Rotschlossen's reaction he knew. He knew the name Christine Stock, or if he did not then he was very paranoid about something else concerning these apparently random but linked events. Perhaps he would find out when he saw Mr Rotschlossen later. *Yes and perhaps I will not survive the meeting with the Rottweiler too...*

With an uncomfortable feeling in the pit of his stomach, Baxter left his office and proceeded in the direction of Karl Rotschlossen's office.

--

Karl had significantly regained his composure by the time he reached his office. He found Baxter pacing nervously in the corridor outside, a clear indicator that he had given too much away on the phone. Baxter turned to face Karl as he noticed him approaching from down the short corridor. The thick, white carpet making his approach noiseless, almost ghostlike in Baxter's mind.

"What is it Baxter? You look like you have seen a ghost." Caught off guard by Rotschlossen's off-hand manner he started to reply but stumbled over his words. "Never mind, never mind. My apologies if I was a little abrupt on the phone, I was in an extremely deep sleep when you called, woke up 'on the wrong side of the bed' as it were."

Baxter nodded, smiling slightly, reassured if not entirely convinced of this explanation. Karl stepped past him, the door automatically unlocking as his handprint was recognised by the door handle, which he twisted and pushed to reveal the office within. The large landscape window taking up much of the back wall was currently blocked by a Venetian blind, had it been open a fantastic view of the city would have been visible. To the right was Karl's old ornamental chestnut desk and comfortable leather chair behind, he seated himself in this and turned his hand towards the uncomfortable straight-backed chairs he kept for visitors to the office. "So what was it you wished to show me?"

Baxter waited a moment as if deciding his response before opening the laptop he had been holding at his side and turning the screen towards Karl. The laptop finished loading from sleep mode and a picture of Christine Stock appeared on the screen. Baxter watched closely for any sign of emotion from Rotschlossen but saw nothing as the picture registered. "As you can see, the girl is missing, probably dead. It appears somebody who is trying to find her has cross-referenced Seba..." Karl looked at him forcefully. "Erm... Sebastian's previous car with this girl. It could be coincidence but only one other car matching the description is within the search area and that car appears to be a different colour to the one that is being looked for."

Karl Rotschlossen looked closely at the picture in front of him and then flicked between the other pages of information open, carefully taking it all in. He had been expecting the photograph and so had not been taken aback at its presence. The drive here had also allowed him time to think over the permutations of the situation. Reading the final pieces of information, Karl turned back to Baxter. "Well done for spotting this Andrew, it is a rare talent of yours to pick up on something so trivial. All this from a search on Sebastian's previous vehicle you say?" Baxter nodded. He felt uncomfortable at the familiar tone Rotschlossen had switched too. Karl sighed, "Well Andrew, it could well be coincidence, this may be linked to the new owner of the car or to this other person with a similar vehicle you said about, or neither." Karl pushed a button on his desk and the blinds shifted to reveal the glimmering city lights, like a blanket of stars sprawled on the ground, stretching in to the distance. He looked out thoughtfully. "This is everything?" Baxter nodded and made to ask something before thinking better of it and deciding to just wait instead but Rotschlossen had noticed. "You were going to say something?"

Baxter felt the knot in his stomach tighten, if he lied Rotschlossen would know, he decided to just bite the bullet and ask anyway. "The girl Sir. Who is she?"

"You ask as if you expect me to know Andrew." Karl turned back to face him. "I am quite sure I do not know who she is." Baxter went to interrupt but Rotschlossen continued. "The name sounded very familiar to me which is why I decided to investigate this matter tonight. The photograph on the other hand has dispelled any familiarity I may have thought existed. You may keep an eye on the situation if you believe it warrants your time but I personally feel no further need to respond to this." He looked the other over with his eyes. Baxter appeared to be deciding how much of what he was being told was true before his eyes cleared and seemed satisfied.

"I have to admit Sir, I was a little worried after the phone call but as you have said it all appears quite coincidental. I shall keep an eye on this just in case but I shall try not to waste any time on it needlessly." He was convinced. He stood up, folding his laptop closed to take with him as he left. Rotschlossen's voice stopped him momentarily in the doorway.

"Oh Andrew."

"Sir?"

"If you could make me a copy of the information you have gathered just so I could double check it with Sebastian."

"Of course Sir. Will there be anything else?"

"Just one more thing, the information you presented to me, it did not have the name of the company doing the checks."

"Not a company Sir, well not exactly. A private investigator, appears he has been on the case pretty much since the girl ran away from home."

"Oh? And his name?"

"Hale Sir. Mitchell Hale. I'll include it in the report when I do a copy of the information."

"If you would Andrew, thank you. That shall be all." Baxter gave a barely perceptible sigh of relief as he left the office, relieved at how well it had gone. Karl turned back to the view of the city. The twinkling lights helping to calm him, helping to order his thoughts. Weighing everything up it seemed he had little choice but to deal with this immediately. Reaching inside his desk he rested his fingers softly over a mound at the back of the drawer. A soft click sounded simultaneously from his now closed office door and the cupboard door at the bottom of his desk as it swung open slightly. Leaning down he removed the matt black phone from its resting place, bulky and old fashioned looking, it lacked any means by which to dial a number, but of course dialling was unnecessary.

"City Industrial Waste Service's which extension please?"

"Extension 58291"

"I have no listing for that number Sir, would you like me to try anyway?"

"If you would, I have no other number."

Soft typing from the other end of the line.

"It appears to be ringing Sir, would you like me to wait and see if it connects?"

"If you could just put me through and I shall wait."

"Very good Sir, you will be redirected back to the switchboard if the connection fails."

"Thank you."

A click, moments silence and then ringing. Several seconds later another click signalled activity on the other end and the ringing stopped.

"City Industrial Waste Service's. This is an internal extension for administration. May I redirect your call to the switchboard?"

"I am having issues regarding the administration of some industrial waste."

"Your name please Sir?"

"Rotschlossen, Karl."

"Please hold."

He turned the receiver away from his ear and waited. A moment later a high pitched screeching noise sounded, after which he placed the receiver against his ear once more.

"Evening Mr Rotschlossen, how may we be of service."

"I wish to arrange a meeting as I may have to outsource some work."

"To whom will you be outsourcing Sir?"

"The Company."

"Very good Sir."

The line clicked and went dead.

Now, to wait.

Karl Rotschlossen sat watching the star like twinkle of the city's lights until the sun rose majestically to chase them away.

Chapter 8

Sebastian moved to clear away the half empty dishes of their meal while Annabel regained her composure. She was not quite sure why she was telling him all this but doing so felt good regardless. Finally somebody seemed to care, to be interested, attentive to what she had to say. That was good enough for her, for now at least. *Why though?* The thought kept haunting her, she scolded herself for distrusting somebody who had been so kind to her and yet the thought of what he would want in return bothered her. *Sex?* He was obviously comfortable enough financially, his car alone was enough to convince her of this, add the penthouse to the top of this and she was convinced he had enough money to have women at his beck and call. *Especially as he's so cute.* She blushed in spite of herself, finding her unexpected emotions overwhelming. *Of course he doesn't want you for sex.* So why? Her mind whirled at the possibilities, what use was she? He had not even known anything about her until he picked her up on the street. Or had he? She shook her head, a new thought occurring to her. Perhaps he was going to sell her or force her in to a life of labour or sell her organs on the black market, perhaps that was how he made his money! It sounded absurd to think it, she shuddered at how ridiculous it would sound to say it out loud but there were rumours of it happening to homeless people all the time, perhaps this was how it started... *Perhaps, perhaps, perhaps. For fuck sake Annabel get a grip!* Her mental scolding sobered her mood. She should just ask him but it seemed so... *rude! Hey thanks for taking me off of that freezing cold street, letting me clean myself, giving me the best meal I've eaten in MY LIFE!!! But I was just wondering if you were going to sell me as a slave on the black market?* Annabel grinned as she considered what his reaction would be at such an outburst.

"Good to see you smiling. Shall we move to the lounge?" He walked up to her, gently placing his hand on the small of her back and guiding her towards the lounge area, upon reaching which he took a seat in the corner of one of the comfortable looking couches and gestured that she should do the same. "Would you like something to drink?" Annabel nodded, almost imperceptibly as she took a seat, realising as she did that she was still wearing only the bathrobe he had supplied her with, being careful to keep her legs together, and covered as much as possible, by the robe. Noticing this as he poured her a glass of wine Sebastian was immediately apologetic. "Oh, I am terribly sorry. Would you like some clothes now? I meant to give you some ages ago."

"No, really it's okay, there's really no urgency just yet." *Not sex then.* She did not know whether to be relieved or dispirited. She leaned forwards taking a pungent glass of red wine from his hand. It smelt lovely and she had to be careful not to down it in one. They sat like that, in silence, for awhile longer. Just enjoying the relaxing feeling of a good meal. Then their eyes met and she could see he was waiting patiently. "Do you want me to continue?"

"Yes. I would like that very much, *but* only if you are ready to do so."

Again she nodded. The familiar barely perceptible movement of her head.

--

She had used the money her mum had given her for new clothes, groceries etc., he had always hated her being given money, saying she was worthless and should earn her own, but that did not matter now. None of it did. She was escaping them. *Both of them!* She did love her mum dearly but she also hated her for bringing *him* in to their lives. Sacrificing her happiness for her own. The money was enough to get her far away, well far enough at least that they would never find her. That's if they even bothered looking. She had it all planned, she would take the train and once she got there, she would use what money she had left to rent a small room while she found a job. Once she did she could use that money to rent a nice flat and then she could do whatever the hell she wanted. The best bit was that no-one would ever hit her again. She promised herself that. In her naivety she had not realised that it was a promise she could not make to herself knowing it would never be broken, she most certainly had not expected it to be broken so soon. She did catch the train, she did rent a room with the money. This was relatively easy but more expensive than she had originally anticipated. Things were a lot more expensive here in the big city than they had been in the quieter northern town she had always known. After much searching she finally found a job cleaning dishes in a small but busy, cafe. The money barely paid for the room she had found to rent but she struggled by and was happy for awhile. But then her luck turned.

Her boss who had always been overly flirty, became oppressive. He argued with his wife every time she visited the cafe and began to arrive at work inebriated more and more often. His presence became intimidating and she strived to avoid him but it was virtually impossible in the small working environment. Inevitably a time arose when they were both alone for closing. To begin with his wife had been there but they had argued and she had left in a rage, he had slammed the door and locked it behind her, leaving just the two of them. She had worked furiously, trying to finish and leave before his temper subsided and his attentions turned to her. She was not quick enough. He bustled around the kitchen for awhile before his attention turned to her and he swaggered over.

"You're a very pretty girl y'know." She smiled amicably, if forcibly, continuing to work. He reached over and touched her back, she jumped, dropping the dish she was holding, it smashing all over the floor. Annabel dropped quickly, away from his grasp, apologising as she hurried to collect the shards of the plate. "Leave it." He grunted roughly. "Come and help me instead." He grabbed her arm laughing, pulling her back up.

"He wanted sex, I should have been surprised it had taken so long to happen really but I had convinced myself it never would because of his wife. I didn't know what to do, if I said no I would lose my job, my flat everything but if I did... what's the difference between that and prostitution?" Annabel looked down. "I felt his hands on me, rough and eager. The old feelings of being wanted returned but so did the memory of how much it had affected my life for the worse. As I struggled with the torment I realised he had torn my work blouse open and I tried to push him away."

He had continued to try his luck, groping at her and ignoring her weak objections. Weak as she was still undecided as to how much worse off she would be without a job. It turned out that fate had made that decision for her. The door was flung open and his wife stood there, her face white with anger. She stormed across the kitchen, ignoring her husbands whining protestations of innocence.

"Darlin', it wasn't me, it was her. She started undressing tellin' me she wanted me."

She had looked in to Annabel's eyes with so many emotions swirling in her own. Anger, disbelief, envy, fear even. It was clear that her husbands grovelling was falling on deaf ears but then her resolve hardened and only anger showed.

"She threw the back of her hand hard across my face. I'd already broken my promise to myself but somehow felt that maybe this time I might actually deserve it. She told me to get out and I did, I ran and never looked back."

About the same time she was notified that her rent was due to increase, she had not had the initiative to arrange a tenants agreement and had not been able to afford paying for months in advance. She either paid or she had to go by the end of the following week. Finding a job was even more difficult this time it seemed and persevere as she might, her attempts all failed. The end of the week came, unlike a new job or the wages owed from the café. She was homeless.

"I was barely 17 and had nowhere to go, so I went nowhere. Nobody wanted to give a job to someone with no address, or telephone number, so I just wandered aimlessly for awhile. My money soon disappeared and I found myself hungry. I met some other people on the streets, eventually another girl about the same age and we kind of banded together to look after each other."

Christine was an imposing character mostly because she was strikingly pretty. Annabel had bonded to her very quickly. A man had tried to steal Annabel's bag while she was sleeping and Christine had seen and stopped him.

"You should be more careful with your stuff at night girl." Annabel smiled thankfully, if a little uncertainly at this unknown helper. "My name is Christine, pleased to make your acquaintance." She reached out her hand towards Annabel, encouraging her to accept it.

"My name is Annabel. Thanks."

"You're welcome girl." Christine walked off in a quick stride and Annabel's temporary joy at having made a new friend subsided as she believed herself mistaken, but Christine then stopped looking at her curiously before asking. "Are you coming with me then?". She walked down a number of back alleys and hidden little passages before they came to a small clearing boxed in almost in it's entirety by fences on each side. It was only about 2 metre's square and was as a result of partitioned fences being built at angles to each other leaving the small space between them. Where one of the fences cornered it left a narrow opening through which they had come. On the floor were some old blankets, boxes, a crate in one corner, a small bag and some other signs somebody had been living there. Christine sat down on the crate. "Home sweet home."

Strangely it did have a homely feel, compared to the urine smelling alleyways at least. It had the impression of being somewhat isolated from the hustle and bustle of the city, as well as the dirt and oppression of homeless life. "Do you live here?"

"Yes girl I do. You can stay too if you want as the other person I shared with has disappeared." Although she said this lightly, her voice wavered slightly and a flicker of sorrow passed behind her eyes. "It's not much but it keeps us safe from most others. It is not easy to find unless you know where to look, so try to make sure no-one follows you here." Annabel nodded dumbly. "You can sleep on that side and if it's cold we can bunch together for warmth although it's quite sheltered from the wind."

"I was 18 at the time, she was a bit older than me and although she had a rough edge to her she came from a richer family than me I always wondered how she had ended up there but we never really discussed it."

Chapter 9

Mitchell Hale sat leafing through the papers his search had yielded as he waited for their return. If he was lucky they would be back soon and he could be in the city before dawn, then rest up for the day before starting where he had left off a year ago. Movement caught his attention on the edge of his peripheral vision and he stopped to look more closely at the couple walking down the street. A man in his mid-forties walking side by side with a girl in her early twenties, if it were not for his hand casually resting on her posterior, you would be mistaken for thinking it may be his daughter.

They walked up the steps to a small house and stopped to kiss briefly in the darkness of the porch, before opening the door and moving inside. Mitchell waited a moment to be sure, then left the car to stealth down the street in the shadows, deliberately positioned between himself and the house, holding his camera tightly concealed within it's case so no glints of reflection would give him away, or draw undue attention to him. The house was relatively compact and had no real privacy. The rooms at the back were above the roof of the back utility room and Mitchell had little trouble pulling himself up on to this and making his way across to the windows.

"...for me! It's beautiful, thanks Tom."

"A pretty thing like you deserves pretty things for herself."

Mitchell could not decide which was more pathetic, his betrayal of his wife or his stupidity in believing this woman was anything but interested in his money and gifts. Some people thought his job was sleazy but he merely saw it as revealing the sleazy actions of others to those who were wronged by them. Mitchell watched carefully from the window as the woman slowly stripped he began taking pictures. He took pictures of her husband watching and of the sex acts the couple shared but as discreetly as possible. No point upsetting his client anymore than was necessary to show her suspicions had been correct. As he lay there gathering his breath and she lay pretending to have to, Mitchell climbed down from the roof and returned to the car. He started the engine and drove away, pushing play on the tape player he refused to update. The sound of his own voice whirred softly from the speakers;

"...the search. Although people had seen Christine, or at least believed they recognised her, she appeared to have been untraceable after a certain point in the day leading many who saw her to reach the conclusion she had a proper place to live, although evidence to support this is non-existent, or at the very least so unlikely to exist outside the sphere of the searches conducted that further resource to investigate would be fruitless." Still, it was strange the way she was never seen sleeping exposed, a girl that pretty would surely have been noticed. *"She was said to have two regular female companions, although one had not been seen recently and the other although a known face was a relatively new companion to Christine at about the time she once again disappeared."* Never did find out who that girl was, perhaps she was the key to it all. He pulled up outside a large house, then after a pause, drove up the driveway to confront his client with the evidence. Although the tape player in his car was an antique the digital SLR he used was top of the range and allowed for pictures to be quickly printed. He parked up and walked to the door with the photographs contained within the envelope in his hand. The guilt he felt when presenting this kind of thing to somebody fired within him as it always did but she deserved to know. Her husband was not acting out of love for someone else, he was acting out of ego for himself. Diminishing his wife's self respect in order to boost his own sense of importance. The inevitable tears would not make it any easier though.

Chapter 10

Annabel looked up at Sebastian. She wanted to continue but felt quite drowsy. It was getting late and the good meal, warm bath and comfort of the couch had done much to relax her. Somehow though she felt obliged to continue and the indecisiveness must have shown on her face as she heard the kindly voice reach out to her again.

"You must be tired, you should stop for now and get some rest. We can continue in the morning." Again he smiled his pleasant smile and without waiting for a response, stood and walked to the corridor. Curiously, Annabel followed, uncertain as to where she would be sleeping but certain it would be more comfortable than the cardboard sheet she had been laying on earlier. "This shall be your room, for the moment at least. If you require anything then you may find me in this room opposite. You shall find some clean clothes that may fit you in the wardrobe but do not worry if they do not as we shall look to furnish you with more appropriate attire tomorrow. You are welcome to eat or drink anything within the kitchen and use the entertainment equipment as you wish but you will find that should you decide to leave while I sleep the lift shall not respond to your calls, therefore you must wake me if you wish to depart. I wish you sweet dreams young Annabel." Softly he kissed the back of her hand and turned, disappearing in to his own room. The warmth the kiss had imbibed on the back of her hand lingered and she felt the overwhelming need to follow him in to his room and request a more intimate appreciation of her but the warmth slowly faded along with her resolve to be replaced by her vacillation. She turned to face the door to the room she would be sleeping in and pushed it purposefully open to reveal the contents. As simply decorated as the other rooms, it contained little more than a bed and a small table at it's side with a lamp and clock. Built in cupboards lined the walls, in which she assumed she would find the promised clothes. She jumped slightly as the door closed itself behind her with a gentle click and she was surprised to note that there was a lock on her side should she wish to secure herself inside. Deciding it was an unnecessary precaution she stepped out of the borrowed slippers and allowed the soft bathrobe to slip from her back. Standing naked in the minimal light cascading from the blinded windows as the moon found purchase in the clearing sky, she took a deep breath and felt free. She strode lithely to the bed and slipped between the clean, crisp sheets. The comfort washed over her and she was instantly asleep.

"So warm and comfortable. Dry. Not aching. So bright." Laying on her back Annabel opened her eyes looking up at the ceiling. She did not panic as although this was a strange place, compared to the past few years it was like awaking in heaven. She also awoke with the events of the previous night at the forefront of her mind. Sitting up slightly she looked towards the foot of the bed in the direction of the light. A breathtaking view was visible between the now open blinds. The sky was a vivid slash of reds and oranges, where the moisture from the downpour still hung heavily in the air. Sunlight glinted off of the rooftops and streets, awash with water even now, hours after the storm had ended. A solitary tear formed in the corner of Annabel's eye, slipping away as it gained weight to leave a rivulet of glimmering wetness in it's wake, reflecting on a smaller scale the view which drew it forth. Annabel sat staring at the beauty but in her heart knew that it was a façade. The gentle arc's, geometric lines and reflected natural colours all worked to hide the unfriendly side of the city's presence. As she looked she thought about some of the horrors the time she had spent on the streets had forced upon her, if not personally then to be seen or heard. *"I can't go back to that."* More tears fell, but slowly.

"Excellent. You are awake."

Sebastian's interruption made her start slightly as she had been so deep in thought. They looked at each other and she was suddenly aware of the wetness on her face. Embarrassed she wiped the tears away with the duvet she was wrapped in, and for a moment their eyes met. The conflict the view had caused within her flickered behind her eyes and he acknowledged it without asking. Suddenly she smelt the food he had brought to her. Egg, sausage and bacon wafted from beneath the heat covers of the tray he carried and freshly squeezed orange juice just visible through a frosted glass, whether frosted from chilling or design she could not yet tell, she realised how hungry she felt, regardless of the excessive meal she had eaten the night previously. It was then that she suddenly became aware of soft music lilting from the corridor beyond the door. Unobtrusive, yet invasive. Foreign but somehow familiar. Sebastian smiled as he realised she had heard the music.

"My apologies, is the music too loud?" Annabel strained to hear it properly, unable to make out what the music was. "I find Mozart quite invigorating in the morning." Annabel wrinkled her nose. "Not a fan? Presently Piano Concerto in E Flat." Annabel raised her eyebrows, a wry look on her face, she had listened to classical music in school and it had always bored her to tears. She would have much rather been listening to something a bit more chart based. Sebastian handed her the tray and turned to leave, he stopped as he reached the door and without turning, spoke. "Come in to the lounge once you have eaten, showered and dressed. I have some people I wish to introduce you too." Annabel could not be certain but she believed there was a flicker of a smile at the corner of his mouth and eyes as he left. Bemused she ate rapidly, eager to discover who these people were. Leaving the tray on the bed, she adorned herself in the robe still abandoned in a crumpled heap on the floor and began searching through the cupboards she had seen the previous night, surprised to find one of them lead to a reasonably spacious en-suite bathroom with a shower, wash basin and toilet. After showering she made her way back to the cupboards and found some jeans and a t-shirt to wear, noting that although the clothes were not new, they were all expensive and designer. Wearing the well made, expensive clothing made her feel at odds with herself. How many meals would these jeans pay for? *Christ these could probably pay rent on a room for a month!* She shook the thoughts from her mind and nervously made her way to the lounge, expecting to find a crowd of people. She was surprised to find only Sebastian.

"Who did you want me to meet?" Perplexed she stood in the middle of the room looking around. Expecting at any moment to be surrounded by inquisitive strangers.

"Take a seat." Sebastian motioned to a seat which Annabel accepted. "Tell me why do you dislike Mozart? Or is it just classical music in general?"

Even more confused by the out of place nature of the question she attempted to answer it. "I don't know. It's just boring I think. They used to make us listen to it at school and I never really thought it was worth wasting time listening to. I like something to sing to."

Sebastian's eye's sparkled and he looked at Annabel thoughtfully, much like a parent would regard a child who had said something amusing. "If I were to suggest to you that I my beliefs on the matter were to the contrary, would you entertain the possibility that I was correct and that your opinion was mistaken?"

She considered this for a moment and then nodded silently, quickly adding. "If you could prove it. I wouldn't just take your word on it. Especially as it is an opinion not a fact."

Sebastian smiled more firmly as if pleased with her response. "Somebody who holds conviction in their own beliefs is somebody worthy of attention." He walked to the music system, like everything else, concealed neatly behind a virtually seamless door. He touched a flat section lightly and the soft music she had earlier heard came flowing majestically from the speakers. "While somebody who is prepared to learn and alter their beliefs accordingly deserves nothing less than respect. All I ask is that you listen and decide whether you like or dislike the music but the choice to listen is of course your own."

Annabel tried to shed her preconceptions as the music floated to her ears. It was okay she guessed. The piano melody was quite good, and the way the instruments seemed to call and answer to each other was almost funny. The music wasn't bad she supposed but did she like it? As the instruments harmonised and reached a crescendo she made her decision. "I do like it."

"It is not boring?"

"There's too much happening for it to be boring, it's almost funny."

"Yes, I too find Mozart's work amusing. For me he is the impertinent child of fun."

"It sounds different now. It seemed more boring at school."

"People who do not have a choice in a matter will rarely find much enjoyment in the partaking."

She nodded her agreement. She was surprised to have not only liked the music but quite enjoyed it. "I guess I hadn't really given it a chance, I just thought it was all crap." The word hung strangely in the air and Annabel immediately wished she could take it back. Swearing in front of Sebastian felt like swearing to a teacher when young, or in a church to a priest. She flushed with embarrassment. "I… I'm sorry. I didn't mean to swear. It just…" Her sentence trailed off as she discovered she could not find the words. *You can take a girl out of the slums but you can't take the slums out of the girl.* She chagrined herself.

"People who swear merely lack the vocabulary to use a suitable alternative; alternately they are too idle to use the vocabulary they have. In to which category would you place yourself?"

She flushed more deeply. She was not stupid, she could have thought of an alternative but hadn't bothered, she made too answer but Sebastian appeared to have moved his attention to something else.

"I…"

"…made a mistake. To err is only human. Do not unnecessarily upset yourself over such a trivial matter." Her face slowly discovered its normal colour and Sebastian closed the cupboard to the control panel. "Now we have enjoyed eggs and Mozart for breakfast, perhaps later you would like Bach, Mahler and Beethoven?" Sebastian leaned forwards slightly and smiled warmly. "Would you like to continue your story now?" A slight chill crept its way up Annabel's spine. She should have expected it she guessed but had still been unprepared. "My apologies, I did not intend to cause you distress."

"No, really it's fine. It's just being here…" She gestured around. "It's almost like my past…" Again she faltered off in to silence.

Sebastian nodded understandingly.

Chapter 11

"Thebe." Steph answered his mobile phone on the first ring. Although asleep just moments ago his voice was not even slightly clouded by disorientation. He was alert and ready. He listened to the short instructions carefully. "Understood."

He dressed quickly but smartly and stepped outside his room at about the same time as Alex Kelsey closed his door down the corridor. They nodded in understanding to each other and walked briskly down the stairs to the waiting elevator. Stepping inside, the doors silently closed and dropped five storeys to the car park without the need of pushing any buttons or making any requests. Everyone inside the complex was closely monitored and their destination was predetermined. The sleek, black Mercedes SLR was parked ready for use as the doors opened, the keys in the ignition. Nobody was going to steal a car here.

"You drive Steph, I'm still a bit muzzy from last night."

"Lightweight."

"Yeah, yeah fuck off." Steph started the engine and Alex, flopped in to the seat beside him. "What's the assignment?"

"Unspecified. We have an appointment with the client in an hour."

"Who's the client?"

"Sebastian."

"Been awhile... Who are we rendezvousing with? Not that fuckin' weirdo Rotsy?"

"Our appointment is with Mr. Rotschlossen, so you may wish to hide that opinion before we get there." Alex grumbled to himself as he tidied his tie. "Cheer up dipshit, at least we can get a nice greasy breakfast."

The thought of some nice unhealthy junk food perked Alex up no end and Steph pulled quickly but smoothly in to the early morning light.

--

The guard on the reception desk looked up at the early visitors who entered through the main doors. One of them was known to him although they rarely visited, the other he had never seen, he only knew they were to be treated with the utmost importance and efficiency. He smiled welcomingly.

"Good morning gentleman. I trust you have an appointment?"

"Certainly. My name is Mr. Smith and my associate Mr. Harris from C.W.M., we have an appointment with Mr. Rotschlossen."

"Very good Sir's." *Smith and Harris my arse.* Gordon lifted the receiver and pushed a button. "Mr. Smith and Mr. Harris here to see you Sir. Very good Sir." He replaced the handset. "Miss Chambers shall be with you shortly to escort you to your appointment."

"Thank you."

Gordon watched apprehensively as the two gentlemen seated themselves in the plush couches of the lobby. The reason for his apprehensiveness lay with the fact that although they were obviously considered to be very important to the company, he could never remember anyone from C.W.M. ever having taken an appointment with Sebastian. *Always with old Karl Rottweiler. The nickname has several meanings of course,* he thought to himself. *There's 'is name obviously but unlike Sebastian he was very cold and authorative towards those with less power than him. Also his loyalty to Sebastian. He was almost obsessively protective of him but what would a man as forthcoming and honest as Sebastian have to be protected from? Everyone liked him pretty much.*

His thoughts were interrupted as Amanda Chambers entered the lobby, smiling playfully at him as she walked past. Rather than stunningly beautiful she was more sultry, with an air of beauty about her. *Definitely attractive...* He knew at his age Amanda was an impossible aspiration but he could dream he supposed...

"Gentlemen, Mr. Rotschlossen shall see you now." Steph and Alex rose to their feet and made their way across the lobby with Amanda. They took the express elevator up to the twelfth floor and then made their way down a corridor to a second elevator to a further unspecified height. All this was completed in polite silence until they arrived outside a large oak door Baxter had dauntingly waited in front of the night previously. "If you would like to take a seat Mr. Rotschlossen shall be out shortly." Without waiting for a reply, Miss Chambers turned on her heel and disappeared back in the direction she had come. There was no need to alert Mr. Rotschlossen to their presence, for he would already be aware of it of course.

The door clicked, Steph and Alex immediately rose to their feet as Karl Rotschlossen opened his office door. "Gentlemen." He held the door ajar inviting them inside, an offer they immediately accepted. Not waiting to be asked they sat in the chairs opposite Rotschlossen's desk and he strode to take position in his own chair opposite them.

"We understand you require the resolution of a certain problem, The Company has sent us to do so." Steph spoke curtly and professionally. He had an unnatural hatred of this man even though he had never met him before. *His eyes betray something when he looks at me. Recognition?*

"You understand correctly." He passed over an edited copy of Baxter's report. "This is the problem I wish you to resolve." Steph took the dossier and slowly leafed through it. "If the problem is resolved within 24 hours then we shall pay twice the normal fee." He hesitated. *He's hiding something.* Steph kept his thoughts to himself. "I… we shall pay an additional bonus for each of you." Steph leaned back in his chair.

"Reason?" Rotschlossen shot him an angry look.

"You do not require a reason. The whole point of The Company is confidentiality."

Steph leaned forwards and met Rotschlossen's angry stare with his own pale gaze. The look sent a creeping chill down his spine but he kept his angry glare on Steph as he began to talk.

"Normally. No, we require no reason." He chose his words carefully. "But in this instance as you are so keen to throw money at the situation then we require a little more insight as to any dangers you may not have mentioned." Rotschlossen regained his composure.

"I see." He continued to return Steph's stare but the familiarity of those eyes made him extremely uneasy. "There are no additional dangers, to yourselves at least but should this... problem be allowed to inflame then it could be very... embarrassing for our company. Company secrets we would rather never reached the light of day." Steph held his gaze a moment longer then stood.

"The Company accepts the contract as requested. We shall return once the problem is resolved." He turned to leave, Alex at his side.

"I would like to add just one more thing, if I may gentlemen." They stopped and turned to face him. "Any and all documentation found is to be returned to me upon your return."

"Agreed."

--

Back downstairs on the way to the car Alex pulled Steph in to an alleyway.

"What the fuck was that about?!?" He stared open-mouthed at Steph. "Asking a client specific details? You'll have us both shot!"

"Didn't it feel a bit weird that he offered over the top for the job?"

"Over the top or not. It's *none of our fucking business!*"

Steph snorted. "I don't trust him."

"I don't trust any of our clients to be perfectly fuckin' honest! But I expect it and don't delve any deeper than necessary. Now what's the real reason you asked him those questions?"

Steph looked in to Alex with the same steely, pale eyed stare he had fixed Rotschlossen with shortly before and had no answers for him. Rotschlossen had looked at him in a way that unsettled him and in a job like this you grew to not only rely upon but trust your instincts implicitly. To do otherwise left you wide open to anything. *Jamie.* He ignored the thought and the unsettled feeling in his stomach and walked back to the car with an angry Alex still in tow.

Chapter 12

Mitchell Hale awoke with a protesting squeak from his mattress. The cheap bed and breakfast he had chosen for his excursion was anything but glamorous. The once ornate wallpaper was mottled with damp and peeling in places. *The carpet could do with some work too.* He acknowledged grimly. Dragging himself out of bed and realising how old he had become, he found his way in to the shower. Glad to see the water was clean and not brown like the shower base implied it would be. Stepping from the shower he felt refreshed and wandered over in his towel to the folder he had that carried information on the Stock case. *The Stock case… Christine… James' daughter.* He shook his head sadly and began leafing through the information he had gathered last night before setting off. The car, rare in the first place, appeared almost unique in the specifications that were obvious upon closer examination of the photograph and he was able to quickly narrow the possibilities down to one. Registered to some industrial company, or more specifically some guy called Sebastian. Quite what he wanted with some homeless girl was beyond him, he was obviously wealthy enough to attract virtually any woman and the press shots he had found of him was enough to grudgingly convince him that what money could not get him, his looks probably could. *12.32.* He had overslept, something else that was becoming more frequent as youth abandoned him.

"Okay, so we've found the likely owner." He spoke aloud, it helped him to focus. "The difficulty now is getting close enough to the owner to question them about it." He mulled the thought over glumly. Although well renowned it seemed for his good naturedness and charity work, meetings with this Sebastian were extremely rare. "Meetings with his colleague Karl Rotschlossen seem a little easier to acquire though…" He scanned through the paperwork and found a telephone number.

"Aisha speaking."

"Would it be possible to speak to Mr. Rotschlossen please?"

"May I ask what it is concerning and who is calling please?"

Mitchell paused for thought for a moment. "My name is Christopher Miles, I am an old school friend of Karl's and wanted to know if he was free for lunch."

"If that is the case Sir then your call would be more appropriately dialled to his private line."

Damn. "The number I have does not appear to be correct, that's why I dialled this one."

There was a silence on the other end as the telephonist contemplated the feasibility of this. *"One moment please."*

--

Rotschlossen's telephone rang interrupting his thoughts. *Odd.* It was very rare for him to be disturbed by an external call, he pondered who it might be as he lifted the receiver. "Rotschlossen speaking."

"My apologies for disturbing you Sir but I have a telephone call from a Christopher Miles claiming to be an old friend of yours."

"I know nobody by the name of Christopher Miles."

"I assumed that would be the case Sir as the number recognition program details the phone the gentleman is calling from as being registered to a Mitchell Hale. I shall get rid off him, apologies for interrupting your time."

Mitchell Hale. Rotschlossen seethed with anger. The men from The Company had barely left, perhaps they would not be quick enough to resolve the situation. He calmed himself. "That is quite alright Aisha, please put the call through and I shall deal with it personally."

"Sir?" In 4 years she had never known Rotschlossen to be so happy to be interrupted even if the caller was a welcome call.

"Today Miss Crawley."

"Immediately Sir. Just one moment." The line clicked and dipped slightly under the strain of the extra connection before the buildings exchange smoothed it out automatically. *"Mr Miles your call is now connected to Mr Rotschlossen, please continue when ready."* Again the soft distortion as Aisha left the call.

"Hello, am I speaking to Mr Rotschlossen."

"You are indeed Mr Hale and to what do I owe the honour of your call?"

"I am calling.." Mitchell stumbled as he realised he had been uncovered already.

"Yes?"

What do I have to lose? *"Regarding Christine Stock."*

"Who may I ask is Christine Stock?"

Nothing. Perhaps he doesn't know anything. "I believe she may have been an acquaintance of your employer. She has disappeared and I am trying to locate where exactly she has disappeared too."

"I know all of Sebastian's acquaintances, personal or otherwise and I do not know of that name."

"Perhaps I could speak to him directly, perhaps you are mis…"

"I think not, it is already bad enough that you have taken up my time unnecessarily."

"If I could just…"

"Good day to you Mr Hale." Rotschlossen calmly replaced the handset. This posed another dilemma, the phone records would undoubtedly be checked and therefore they needed editing. The last thing he needed was some intruding police presence investigating why this annoyance contacted him before… *Well before.* Rotschlossen returned to staring anxiously out of his window.

--

Shit! Mitchell looked at the mobile phone he clasped angrily. "Okay, it's not a complete loss. Think about what you have learnt from the call." He sat on the edge of the bed. "Rotschlossen knew who I was before he took the call." *Probably caller ID or something.* "If he knew my name before I spoke to him then why did he take my call?" *Curiosity? Maybe, but more than that.* "He knew or recognised my name." *Good. Why would he though? Coincidence? No.* "Maybe it's a company policy to keep a close watch on anyone investigating their boss." The idea definitely seemed feasible but he was still not convinced. *Then why talk to me? If they knew I was investigating the owner of the car then surely they knew what else I had been investigating.* Mitchell Hale sat staring at the picture he had pinned to the wall in front of him uncomfortably deciding his next step. Christine's pale skin was a sharp contrast to the sleek black of the car she was leaning in to.

Chapter 13

Steph and Alex sat in their car down a dark side alley where they would not be noticed. Trading the vulgar SLK for a more innocuous Vauxhall Vectra.

"So we can rule out a UCBT then."

"Check. Draw too much attention, same goes for the Druganov." Alex looked ruefully at the boot that housed both the plastic explosives for the under-car booby trap and the 7.62mm sniper rifle.

"Well the front is too open to scale. Internal entry?"

"Yeah but explosive entry is out too I'm afraid." Laughing to themselves they continued to mull it over, their thoughts interrupted by Steph's mobile. "Thebe." The voice on the other end spoke quickly and not loudly enough for Alex to overhear. "Understood." He hung up.

"Problem?"

"Kind of…"

"He didn't mention your interrogation of the client?" Alex paled noticeably.

"No but our problem did just make a phone call to him." Steph set his jaw. "In and out. Short and sweet. No mess and discreet."

"How though?"

"Like this."

--

The Vectra casually pulled up outside the bed and breakfast. A man stepped from the car and quickly entered the building as the car pulled away. He made his way past the fat, balding owner. Parked in front of the television at the reception desk, unmoving as he strolled past. Upon reaching the stairs he quickly sprinted up them, sticking to the sides where they were less likely to squeak and give him away. It was early afternoon but nobody was about as he progressed up three flights to the floor he required. *Number 36.* The room was already known to him of course, the task in itself was easy, it was just the covertness that made it a challenge. *And what a challenge.* A middle aged man and a young girl fell out of one of the rooms laughing and joking. From their attire he guessed as to what her profession was and wondered momentarily if the rest of the guys at the office spent their lunch times the same way. He shielded himself in a doorway, pretending to have difficulty with the lock. They continued past without much notice, him with an air of avoidance, her with a momentarily appraising eye of his form. *The difficulty would be unsuspicious entry.* He reminded himself of the task, chastising himself for not acquiring a spare key from reception. *But that would mean another witness.* He contented himself to working his way further down the corridor. *I could pick the lock. NO! Stick to the plan. Rule number one, always stick to the plan until it becomes unfeasible to do so.* He looked once more down the corridor, he was close now. He walked up to the door. Checked his watch. *5 seconds... 3... 2... 1...* He knocked loudly on the door.

"Sarah I know you're in there. Open up." Jumping at the sudden commotion Mitchell Hale looked up at the door.

"There's no-one here called Sarah." He called back agitatedly. More bangs.

"Don't lie to me. I know she's in there." Mitchell sighed, rising to his feet he walked towards the door. The poor guy sounded upset, although his bangs were insistent his voice remained low, if determined. "Please Sarah, just let me in." Mitchell reached up and unlocked the door. It immediately swung in and a man stood there taking up the entire doorway. "Where is she?"

"Look here, I already told you...!"

"Don't lie to me." The man pushed past moving to look under the bed, ignoring Mitchell's objections. He proceeded to look in the wardrobe and then went to the bathroom. Mitchell stood where he was patiently waiting for him to find nothing, he continued looking at the entrance to the bathroom but after several minutes the man failed to return from it. Puzzled, Mitchell closed the door to his room to stop any further random intrusions from crazy people entering and walked towards the bathroom to find out what had happened to his unexpected visitor.

Chapter 14

Annabel sat on the dirty blankets laying on the floor. "So how long have you lived here then?"

Christine shrugged. "Can't really remember to be honest girl." She smiled, wry but sincere all the same. "Time doesn't have heaps of meaning these days."

"I know the feeling." Annabel looked around her. "Where did your friend go?"

"Hmm?" Christine looked up distractedly.

"The friend you mentioned, you said she disappeared. What makes you think she disappeared and didn't just leave?"

Christine looked uncertain. "She was a nice girl. We were pretty close. Well I thought so... She wouldn't just up and leave me. We had plans, we were going to get out of here." Annabel smiled understandingly and Christine looked back with a hard glare. "It's not what you think. It's not denial. She left stuff here she never would have left behind. See for yourself." She gestured to the corner where a bag and some other things lay. "Look I invited you here to help you girl, not to be interrogated and judged like *they* do. You can always clear off again!"

"No, no I'm sorry. I just... I wondered..." But she couldn't find the words.

"It's okay girl. I didn't mean to get angry with you, I only wanted to help you and for you to ask so many questions about her. It hurts you know." Annabel nodded. "I don't understand why she went, or why someone would take her?"

"Perhaps she went back to her family?"

"Unlikely, she hated most of her family. There was a brother but she hadn't seen or heard from him for ages before she left. I think she hated him less than the rest, more resented him for finding a way out and not helping her too."

"What do you mean?"

"I don't know girl, she was always quite vague about it all but bare this in mind. This place here, it's pretty safe but this area..." She stopped, lowering her voice without meaning too. Annabel leaned closer so not to miss anything. "...People disappear."

"What do you mean?"

"That's why I brought you in from that alleyway. I saw you a few days ago but didn't know whether I could trust you to be here with me. But it's not safe out there. Girls like us just seem to vanish around here, if it weren't for this place I would have cleared out ages ago."

Annabel nodded in agreement without further questions. People disappeared on the streets all the time but who cares about some homeless nobody? It's not like they have anyone to realise they didn't return to their doorway that night. *Or anyone to care whether they did.* She thought bitterly. She picked up the bag. "May I?"

"Go ahead. She's not coming back." Christine slumped to the floor, her back against the fence. The bag contained nothing of any worth really. Some old clothes, some bits of make-up, trinkets, a couple of photos of her and Christine. Annabel held it up to Christine and she nodded. "That's her." And a photograph of some guy. "Her brother." Christine acknowledged simply. The pale blue eyes stared solemnly out of the photograph at her. Although obviously young, no more than fourteen or fifteen, his eyes had a look of someone much older. She carefully replaced the items back in the bag, suddenly feeling a little ashamed at having unceremoniously rifled through them. With a slight reverence she replaced the bag back where she had found it and looked apologetically at Christine. She smiled warmly. "As I said, she's not coming back."

--

Annabel looked up at Sebastian who had been listening intently as she told of her meeting with Christine. "Christine was the first and only person to show me any real kindness since I was on the streets. Well except…" Her eyes met his for a moment and she immediately dropped them blushing slightly. This in itself making her blush even more deeply. "Christine was brash and never exactly let me get close but there was a bond between us, at least I thought so… No. There was. People disappear all the time on the streets the difference between it happening out there and in here is that in here there are people to notice. If I disappeared right now, who would notice? You would assume I had just upped and left and no-one would care but you!" She said it almost accusingly, jealously even? "You. With your nice apartment and fancy clothes and chauffeur and job and company and employees and… and…" She started to cry. "People don't realise. It's better to be hated and missed than not be noticed at all." Sebastian passed her a box of tissues, lightly fragranced with some sort of balm she noticed, as she dried her eyes and blew her nose as softly as she could. "I'm sorry. I didn't mean to take it out on you."

Sebastian smiled his understanding, father-like smile. "It really is fine. I understand the anger that people feel towards people like I. I was born with a silver spoon in my mouth so to speak but every walk of life has it's trials and tribulations. It has its ups and its down, its hardships and its pleasures." He stopped. A pensive look on his face. "Their failures and their successes."

Annabel thought about this. "I guess we all do." She agreed. "I never thought Christine would abandon me though."

--

Annabel and Christine wandered down the street side by side. Their friendship gave each of them a new lease of life, and confidence. Whether that was a good thing or a bad thing was yet to be seen but for the moment things were on the up. They spent the morning sorting through boxes of bananas in exchange for a few pounds from the shop owner.

"Catch!"

Annabel looked up and caught the brown thing flying towards her. Not realising until the last second as the over-ripe banana squished between her fingers.

"Ewww. Christine that is gross." She flicked her fingers at Christine and laughed as it spattered over her face.

"Ewww. You silly mare. That went in my mouth that did!" She started pretending to choke as if on something highly toxic, dramatically throwing her hands to her throat and rocking from one side to the other. "I'm... dying... can't... breathe..." She collapsed in to Annabel's arms. Annabel took on a look of dramatic regret.

"Oh Christine. I'm so sorry I poisoned you. How can I ever make up this horrible thing I've done to you!" It was at this point her strength gave out and they both collapsed in to a heap on to the grimy floor. Upon completion of their task, the shop owner gave them twice what he said he would after passing a pitying eye over them. They smiled gratefully and discussed what to do with their new found wealth. Everything was imagined from buying a fancy apartment in one of the rich parts of the city to buying a new wardrobe and being 'discovered' by a Hollywood talent scout. In the end the reality was a meal from a take-away van that supplied the lunchtime workers with their food. Buying a selection of groceries from a supermarket would have been a more fruitful use of the money, in more senses of the word than one but where would they cook the food they had bought? They did buy some fresh fruit with the money and kept the rest for the following day. You couldn't always count on being able to find work and you couldn't always count on being paid for the work either.

Things continued like this for a few months and Annabel began to feel a sense of belonging. The enclosed shelter of the fences gave her a sense of security and safety. For the next few months Annabel slept more soundly than she had in a long time. The worries about awaking to find a drunken stranger standing over her receded in to the shadows as did the fears that she might not wake up at all. It was not comfortable in the traditional sense but somehow, it was home. Annabel and Christine would spend the daytime trying to gather some money, whether individually or together and the night was spent in the security of their little oasis of solitude away from the dangers.

Until one night Christine failed to return. Annabel sat waiting late in to the night but still there was no sign. Eventually she fell asleep certain Christine would wake her upon her return or that she would be asleep next to her when she woke.

But she did not wake her, and she was not there when she awoke.

It was several days before Annabel faced the reality. Christine was not coming back. At first she was enraged, completely fuming that Christine had abandoned her, then she was afraid. Christine would not leave her, not without saying goodbye. She had asked after her of course but few had seen her. Even a pretty young blonde received little attention when she was homeless and dressed in dirty rags. As the days wore on she found no sign of her and stories that conflicted. Somebody thought they might have seen her catching a train, another thought they had seen her talking to a man in a car, some said they had seen her asking the grocer if he had more work and yet another thought he had seen her being arrested. Secretly she hoped the last to be true, although she would not admit it to even herself. If Christine had been arrested for whatever reason at least she was safe. *And she hasn't abandoned me.* The thought brought fresh tears to her eyes. The days became long and drawn out inevitably becoming weeks and then months. Still no Christine. The only security in her life was her and Christine's little oasis of safety. *My oasis of safety.* She thought bitterly. Even with the security of this though, a profound fear had sown it's seed within the pit of her stomach, planted deep within the rich soil of her subconscious, it scared her before she fully understood exactly what *it* was. Christine had been brash and in control, certainly much stronger than she considered herself. From their infrequent discussions about Jamie she had the impression that she too had been more than a timid little girl and if anything had sounded even more resilient than Christine. This could be down to a certain amount of exaggeration on Christine's behalf but she felt certain it must be true to a certain degree. *What chance do I stand?* Even with the safety of the little oasis both Christine and Jamie before her had been swallowed by the darker side of the city, was she going to be next? Furthermore she realised that Jamie's disappearance had been as upsetting to Christine as Christine's disappearance had been to her. Christine's reactions to certain comments and questions reflected her own reactions and feelings concerning Christine. As she wandered back towards the oasis in the gathering dusk she began to reconsider whether it was truly as safe as they had all believed. Perhaps someone else knew about the place and was doing something to the people who sheltered there. Shaking her head solemnly she kept it down as she neared her destination, not noticing the two shadows behind her even though they were following in a less than stealthy fashion. Later when she reconsidered this she realised she had known they were there but at the time was too lost in her own thoughts to realise the potential danger.

Annabel squeezed through the small gap in to the shelter, still expecting to see Christine's familiar face, even though it had been a few months since her disappearance. She collapsed disheartened to the floor, tired and alone. She closed her eyes and relaxed to go to sleep. Then she heard it. A scraping noise, the sound of someone squeezing through the gap. *Christine!* She sat up instantly and spun expecting to see Christine and her roguish grin but was immediately disappointed instead to be met with a dishevelled and drunken leer.

"'Ello young'un. What's a pretty one like you doin' out'ere in the cold?" He laughed dangerously and another figure slipped from the gap behind him. "See Baz. I told yer' I saw her go in 'ere. How about I help warm you up?" He started forwards and Annabel backed against the fence. *Is this what happened to Christine and Jamie?* She suddenly realised that the same characteristics that had offered so much protection now provided no route of escape. The drunk lunged for her and she felt his grimy hands grip her wrist, his other hand trying to find a way under her top. She tried to scream and found the second man had clamped his hand around her mouth, his acrid breath making it even harder for her to breathe. She felt nauseous and dizzy as panic rushed through her body in waves. She tried to calm herself. The man, 'Baz', who had clamped her mouth with his hand, was fumbling with the belt and fastenings on his grimy jeans. The other man who had tried to get inside her top had now turned his attention instead to trying to force his hand down her jeans and to her increasing distress was having more success than he had been having with her top. She fumbled around with her free hands and found purchase on something hard and smooth. Annabel felt a slither of hope as she realised it was a glass drinks bottle she had finished with that morning. Gripping it as tightly as she could, she swung it with all her strength at the head in front of her. The bottle connected with a resound clunk, smashing on impact. Without thinking about what she was doing she thrust forwards with the shards of the broken bottle in to the now exposed groin of the man holding his hand over her mouth. He let go with a roar, tripping over his now unconscious friend in the confined space, crashing against the fence. Annabel scrambled towards the gap as an opportunity of escape presented itself. Fresh panic raced through her as a hand clasped her ankle and an angry face appeared in the gap, blood flowing freely down it. She spun and kicked as hard as she could physically manage in to the face. The hand released her and she scrambled away, the screams of pain and anguish fading in to the noise of the city as the distance increased. The oasis was safe no more and once again she found herself alone, afraid and with nowhere to go.

Chapter 15

Karl replaced the receiver. The Company had been informed of the phone call, now he needed to make certain the phone call ceased to exist. The dilemma being that should even the smallest part be overlooked then the ensuing investigation, should there *be* an investigation, would arise immediate suspicion as to why the records had been so intricately and professionally erased. Rotschlossen thought through the process. *The Company are incredibly efficient at such tasks but even the most efficient people make mistakes.* Situations like this were their speciality but never before had a situation been so important. So close to home as it were. He could of course request the services of some of their own staff, in fact Baxter would no doubt be able to remedy the problem in less than an hour but that would mean drawing more attention to the situation. *It would be best to leave it in the hands of the company.* What about their representative though? *Those familiar eyes. The way he cornered me for further information.* Karl was nervous, as he had been only once before that he could recall in his lifetime.

--

Immediately he could feel something was wrong. He entered with much less caution than his instincts informed him too but only one thought was in his mind. *Sebastian.* His eyes darted hurriedly around the room but could not directly find the cause of his uneasiness. It was at this moment that two things came to his attention in the same instant. The bed was empty and the windows were not closed properly. The combination of the slight autumn chill coming from the tiny crack of the open window in addition to the silent and therefore empty room had alerted his instincts long before his senses.

Karl pulled his driving gloves from his pocket and slipped them on in one fluid, practised movement as he sprinted towards the window. Pulling the window open he sprang in to the frame and lithely jumped to the ground floor to land next to the indentations from a ladder in the gravel. There were no tyre marks evident but footprints were legible leading towards the sprawling gardens and on, in to the moist grasses and beyond to the trees. All of this he observed without stopping as he rapidly headed in the direction the footprints lead. *Sebastian.* The thought entered his mind again, momentarily distracting him before filling him with renewed vigour as he increased his already suicidal pace in pursuit, the single-mindedness of which bordered on insanity. It had been his responsibility to keep him safe and he had failed. He must redeem himself. Failure was certainly not an option and not even would his own death excuse him should he do so.

He entered the trees at speed but was quick to slow and move quickly but stealthily, among them. The ground would be difficult to traverse, especially with an unwilling companion accompanying them. He bounded from the ground to roots to fallen trees without slowing, his graceful determinedness would have been intimidating beyond comprehension should anyone have been able to witness it. A sound. He stopped. A door closing to a vehicle.

Abandoning any and all furtiveness, he careened through the brush and foliage with disregard for nature's strength and his own safety. Still he maintained the grace but the stealth had been replaced with a sense of purpose and rage. *Sebastian.* Again the thought, they could not be allowed to escape. He came through the trees on to a little known about track that ran to the edge of the property. Even though it was known only to a few, a special security patrol was normally employed to keep watch over it and certain other areas of the estate. A black van stood facing him about 20ft away and he found himself caught in the beams of the headlights. He charged at the van as if it were nothing more than a frightened rabbit. The astounded driver reacted by dropping the clutch and flooring the accelerator. Everyone was on board, only this man stood in their way. As both parties picked up speed, Karl launched himself in to the air at the last moment, twisting in the air and meeting the windshield of the van with his shoulder. If the van had been on tarmac instead of an uneven slippery track then death would have met him immediately. Instead the collision resulted in the windshield cracking as it met the muscle and sinew of the toned body. Karl lay on the windshield, winded but hanging on as the driver continued to accelerate forwards. Sounds of distress came from inside and in a moment of inspiration the driver locked the brakes sending Karl flying forwards in to the underbrush. He dragged himself first to his knees and then to his feet as the brake lights faded in to the distance. He had seen the number plate and the face of the driver, him having been foolish enough to not deem a mask as necessary. He would pay for that lapse of judgement. They would all pay.

--

The buzzer sounded quietly and a light on his desk flashed simultaneously rudely disturbing his ruminations. Turning his attention to the present he pushed the button to allow the speakerphone a voice. "Yes?"

"Apologies Sir. Will Sebastian be in work today as there are a few calls he wished to make to clients."

Sebastian. "My understanding is that he shall be in at some point later this afternoon."

"Very good Sir." The voice wavered slightly and the connection remained open.

"There was something else?"

"Sir. If I am not being too intrusive Sir."

"Yes?"

"Are you okay..? You do not quite seem yourself today."

Rotschlossen started. He could not remember anybody ever having enquired after his health before, mostly people avoided him and hoped any health problems were terminal. He doubted it was concern for himself, more a fear of what could potentially befall them should he be in a foul mood. He respected them for asking though. "I am fine." Begrudgingly adding. "Thank you." He reached down to the panel and cut the voice off before it could comment further. The action bringing a very slight twinge from his shoulder. *It has not concerned me in years.* He moved his shoulder smoothly, feeling nothing. Nothing but the distant memories of that time. *Sebastian.*

--

The word died before it reached his lips and with it the momentary emotion. He turned feeling the numbness in his shoulder but ignoring it. In order to get in to the estate they would have to bypass security and that was not possible. Without help.

Karl picked up speed as he headed back towards the house, if they had been able to get in they would be able to get out again. Pursuing the vehicle would be pointless, pursuing the person who had allowed them entry would be far easier. He advanced purposefully on the security room upon re-entering the house. As he approached the door opened to a familiar face, a face not quite quick enough to hide the look of fear and surprise that briefly crossed it.

"Karl! What a nice surprise! What are you doing up so…" He never had the chance to finish his sentence as Karl's fist connected squarely with his jaw, dropping him with a resounding clump. This one. He helped them. He knew it without reason. He took a roll of duct tape from the shelves and bound his captive's hands and wrists, slamming his limp body against the wall as it showed the first signs of stirring.

"Karl! What the hell are you doing?"

His voice stank of fear, lies and betrayal.

"Malcolm. Where is Sebastian." His voice remained calm, his eyes flared dangerously. Malcolm Campbell stuttered badly as he tried desperately to escape Karl's accusing eyes. "I… I don't… I." *Pain. Such incredible pain.* Malcolm released a scream as Karl forced a pen in between his knuckles, unable to move his arms from the steely grip.

"Sebastian." Karl twisted the pen sharply. Another scream.

Malcolm looked in to the unrelenting eyes with fear and saw only insanity looking back at him. His mind was still reeling from the overwhelming force of the situation. With absolutely no evidence Karl had hit him, bound him and was now torturing him excruciatingly. This alone was enough to put the very fear of God in him, the fact that Karl was right feared him even more. "Please Karl. I don't know, what you're…" Another scream. He breathed deeply, tears flowing freely down his face. He looked in to the unrelenting eyes and broke. "They didn't tell me." He dropped his head in shame. Karl grabbed his chin and forced him to look in to his eyes.

"What do you know?"

"Only the time. I made sure they would be able to…" He looked fearfully in to Karl's face unable to look away. "…get in unnoticed by the other guards."

"What else?"

"Nothing else. I…" Malcolm felt the pen push deep in to his flesh again. Searing pain somehow racking his entire body. By the time Karl had finished Malcolm was sat in a pool of his own urine and everything he knew, Karl knew. As he turned to leave he was met by two security guards and Sebastian's Father.

"Karl. What is the meaning of this?"

"My apologies Sir. Sebastian is gone." He kept walking.

"Where are you going?"

He stopped as if puzzled. "To fetch Sebastian of course." With that he turned and continued walking.

--

He sat in the Range Rover. The baton he had relieved Malcolm of in the passenger seat. Calmly he started the engine and drove from the garage. Karl used the in-car phone to contact an associate, the licence plate, it turned out was not registered, the address Malcolm had given him however was valid and was being rented temporarily in a company name. Karl pulled up opposite the warehouse that resided in the space the address specified. It was pretty much in darkness, except for one window at the front.

Karl exited the vehicle soundlessly and crept in the shadows towards the warehouse, the baton strapped firmly to his back. Upon reaching the corner of the building he tested the strength of the guttering, pulling against it firmly before ascending hand over hand towards the roof. He pulled himself over the edge and scanned the roof for a way in. The night was clear and the roof well lit. An entrance was clearly visible towards the rear of the building, so slowly, he made his way across the roof, careful not to alert those beneath him to his presence. At the door he checked it and was not surprised to find it locked... but not well. He quickly gained entry and proceeded inside. Darkness enveloped him.

When Karl stepped back outside via the ground floor entrance, the light was no longer on. The warehouse was in silence and the baton he held in his hand was smeared with blood. Nestled against his chest, carried in the crook of his injured arm, regardless of the searing pain it was now causing him, lay Sebastian.

--

It had been due to his incompetence that Sebastian had ever been placed in danger that first time and now it was due to his incompetence again that Sebastian faced danger, albeit of a different variety. He reflected and knew that the little 'excursions' like the one involving Christine had always placed Sebastian in this danger but never before had it actually resulted in a situation like this. *Prevention is better than cure.* He chastised himself and sat heavily in his chair. The company had not called but then perhaps there had not been enough time. *Discretion is paramount to success in such things, whereas haste and conspicuous action was tantamount to failure.* His thoughts did little to comfort him.

Chapter 16

Annabel sat softly weeping. She had failed to realise that Sebastian had moved in order to be able to embrace her comfortingly. He held her close against his chest and the tears flowed freely. She coughed, clearing her throat and tried to regain her composure.

"I'm fine." Upon seeing the doubt in his eyes she added, "Really. I'm okay." She attempted a smile and he sat back in the crook of the couch. "After that, I was kind of lost I guess. I was so afraid they would catch me but I couldn't help but go back. It took me a few days to get the courage but I did but..." She faltered. "It wasn't the same. The place stank of urine and there was dried blood in places. I left it and went back to sleeping in alleyways but nearby because, well, Christine, you know?" Sebastian nodded with the same comforting fatherly air. She wondered how she knew it was fatherly and decided it was a memory from her childhood of her real father, the only other man who had truly been kind to her. "That's pretty much it until you found me. I thought I was going to die. I was so cold when you spoke to me, I... I..." She looked up at him, deep sorrow in her eyes but also gratitude. "I really believe you saved my life last night." Sebastian raised an eyebrow thoughtfully, a look of scepticism upon his face. "It's true!"

"We shall see. It is one thing to prevent somebody from dying but it is quite another to save somebody's life." He hid his amusement as she looked at him quizzically. "You, young Annabel are still breathing and your heart continues to beat within your chest but that is not life. To have life you are required to live. As to whether I am the one who is responsible for the former is a matter of debate but we shall see what we can do about helping you realise the difference between being alive and living."

"I don't think I understand what you mean but I do still think it's you I need to thank for still being alive. Christine was much stronger than me and from what she said about Jamie, she was even stronger but they both disappeared, or perhaps they left." She said the last bit flatly, thick resentment in her voice.

"Try not to belittle yourself; you may be stronger than you consider yourself to be."

Annabel looked up at him, a question flashing in to her head, begging to be asked but ashamed to do it aloud. She took a deep breath; "Why *did* you pick me up from the streets?" She sat in silence, watching as Sebastian appeared to consider the question.

"I was born to an extremely wealthy family. We have always been a family at the forefront of advances, as far back as the industrial revolution and so it continues with me and what my family company has evolved in to. To see something so frail upon the streets, so near to death, it fills me with a sense of melancholy. Not guilt as it is not my fault that people such as you live in such conditions but sadness all the same. For all my wealth I could not afford to help every person in need throughout the world but I do try to help. If I cannot help every person I shall strive to help those I can, I merely let fate guide me in my decision."

Although it was the answer she had hoped to hear she could hardly believe it was true; he had picked her up because he was being *nice*. The idea seemed very silly but romantic all the same. A noise rang out startling her from the romanticism clouding her thoughts.

"If you will excuse me momentarily, that is the internal phone." Sebastian stood and looked down at Annabel. He walked across the room with guile and strength befitting his personality; reaching a handset by the door he lifted it to his ear.

"Hello, this is Sebastian."

"Begging your pardon Sir, I am here to convey you to work as requested."

"Ah yes. Very good Samuel, I must apologise for I have allowed time to slip away from me this morning. I shall be down momentarily."

"No apology is necessary Sir. Take as much time as is required."
Sebastian replaced the handset and turned to Annabel. To miss work today
was unquestionable as a few specific matters required his attention. Karl could
always step in on his behalf but to act in such a manner was not appropriate
for a person in a position of power such as Sebastian's. *Lead by example
Sebastian.* The voice of his father resonated strongly in his thoughts. *The
dilemma that presents itself of course is what to do with Miss Annabel.* Leave
her here and he may find he no longer has any possessions upon his return,
although he considered this to be highly unlikely it was not a risk he would be
willing to accept freely. She would have to call down as she would not have
the facility to operate the lift by herself, however he could hardly request that
reception ignore any requests for her to do so. To take her to the office was of
course an option but in doing so questions would be asked as to her origins
and purpose. Questions they would both find uncomfortable answering. *It is
rare that any individual would question my actions.* Sebastian deliberated the
options and determined that Annabel would have to accompany him to the
office. Other arrangements should have been made but it was too late to do so
and therefore a decision that would resolve the situation was required.
Annabel shall have to accompany me to the office. "Annabel, I must go in to
work for a few hours." She looked up at him, her demeanour likeable to that of
a rabbit he thought.

"Okay."

She said the word with uncertainty he noticed, he would be required to clarify.
"I would like it very much if you were to escort me there as it would be most
discourteous of me to leave a guest here all alone." He watched Annabel
carefully for her reaction, she appeared both shy and surprised by his request
but not opposed to it. He looked to her feet. "Could you find no suitable
footwear in the closets?"

"No they were all the wrong size." She shrugged indifferently. "I can
just wear my shoes."

"What size shoes would you generally wear?"

"My old shoes were size 4 but they were a little tight and stretched from wearing them so long."

Sebastian considered this. "In that case, wear the slippers you currently have upon your feet and I shall seek a solution to meet us at our destination."

--

The car that awaited them was different to the one that had driven them yesterday evening. It was a big car Annabel didn't know but it was still very comfortable she decided. As she had stepped outside from the warmth of the building she shuddered, both with the cold and the thought that she had been forced to sleep outside in this until just yesterday. She thought sadly of the other homeless people who were not as lucky as she was. The car ride was pleasant enough but she felt very silly wearing pink slippers in the car. Sebastian had changed in to a suit that looked magnificent. It wasn't flashy she thought but the cut of the suit and the way it hung on Sebastian was remarkable. The car pulled up outside a towering building that succeeded in dominating those surrounding it without being taller than some. The architecture was compelling but minimalist. The building truly looked like somewhere Sebastian owned and worked.

The car door was opened by a doorman from the buildings entrance but rather than holding the door open for Annabel and Sebastian to exit the vehicle, he dropped to one knee and knelt before Annabel with three small boxes in his hands. "As requested Sir."

"My thanks to you Peter."

"My pleasure Sir, if madam pleases?" He held out the boxes to Annabel and she slowly opened one of them, she laughed in surprise as true to his word Sebastian had arranged for a solution at their destination. The boxes contained identical pairs of sports shoes, incrementing in size. The first pair, the size 4's, was too tight but the second pair fitted comfortably. "Very good madam." He collected the boxes and wrapping, then proceeded to stand beside the open door allowing Annabel to step out and Sebastian to follow. "Sir you should have allowed me to open your door also."

Sebastian smiled the now familiar comforting smile. "To do so would have been unnecessary Peter and my awareness that you would have felt better doing so is as agreeable for me as if you had waited on me."

"Thank you Sir." Peter beamed proudly and walked them to the doors, although the entrance on most of the neighbouring businesses were now fitted with electric doors, the older doors had remained here and Peter held one open while maintaining his hold and balance of the boxes he had taken from Annabel.

Annabel entered the lobby and stood, where a Mr Smith and Mr Harris had stood barely a few hours previously, and stared in wonder at the grandeur of the room. It had the same subtle strength that everything she had seen of Sebastian's had. Not blunt and showy but delicate and complimentary, she decided it was one of the most breathtaking rooms she had ever been in.

"Good morning to you Gordon."

"Good morning Sir." Gordon sat up even straighter than he had been prior to Sebastian's arrival.

"Relax Gordon; you shall hurt your back if you put strain on it so."

"Yes Sir." He relaxed, but only slightly.

"Do I have any messages?"

"Just the one you have been expecting Sir. The gentleman from Oechsle is expecting your call."

"Thank you Gordon."

As they walked past Gordon and passed other people on their route to wherever it was that Sebastian was taking them, Annabel noticed that everybody greeted Sebastian warmly, even if in a hurry so only a curt nod could be afforded. More remarkable to her mind was that Sebastian replied in greeting to every person by name, even to an obviously intimidated delivery boy in his early teens working the weekends for some extra money, but at the warmth of greeting from Sebastian he relaxed noticeably, flushing slightly at the use of his name.

"Do you know everyone who works here?"

"I do."

"How many people work here?"

"Three… Good morning Ian, three thousand, two hundred and seventy three if memory serves me correctly and approximately one hundred or so regular visitors." Annabel was so shocked she stopped immediately, her mouth hanging open as her jaw had dropped. "Are you okay?" He asked with genuine concern. She realised she must look pretty strange stood there with her mouth wide open.

"Yes, I… I guess I am just… surprised?" She couldn't quite explain it herself but she thought the idea that Sebastian knew all the people in the building was overwhelming. "Why do you know them all?"

"I interview everybody who works for the company personally, so I have met everyone who works here at least once before."

"Yes but why do you bother to? It must be very difficult to remember everyone's name."

It was Sebastian's turn to stop. He turned and looked at Annabel, bemusement etched in to every corner of his face. "Every person who works here knows who I am and my name, is it not good manners that I extend the same courtesy to each of them?" He turned and continued walking and Annabel had to jog slightly to catch back up with him. She wanted to tell him that everyone knowing him was different but she couldn't quite find the words to explain why. As they finally came to some huge doors with sentries at either side the thoughts were lost completely in the shadow of the spectacle that met her. The lift they had just taken had brought them to a very narrow passageway, just wide enough for two people to walk down side by side. At the end of the passage, where they now stood the way forward opened out in to a T shape and as well as the two sentries stood either side of the doors, a further sentry could be seen stood against the wall of either arm of the T. Even more surprisingly though was that all four men were carrying firearms. Annabel was no expert and knew little more than she had seen on TV but she was certain that as well as the pistols the other guns they carried were some sort of machine gun. She looked to Sebastian, her mouth once more hanging open in question.

"You have a question?"

She looked around. "These men…"

"Yes?" Sebastian was looking bemused again.

She could just about bring herself to say it but managed to whisper. *"They have guns!"*

Sebastian looked down at Annabel with the slightest air of pity but then realised her naivety and instead smiled warmly. "Of course they carry guns Annabel."

"Is that *legal*?" She seemed astonished that Sebastian had admitted it even though she could see them with her own eyes.

"The firearms we have stocked within the building are known to the relevant authorities and as we do a substantial amount of work for said authorities it is important to them that we are as secure as is possible, therefore the firearms are allowed. Come, I require something from my office." He flashed his warm smile and walked towards the double doors of his office. Again the design was simple and yet luxurious. Made from fine oak they gave the impression that mother nature herself had planted and nurtured the doors in to existence rather than them having been placed by a builder or carpenter. Sebastian greeted the four sentries by name and pushed open the doors to his office. A slight gesture of his head safe guarded Annabel's passage without her being aware he had done so. Had he not then instead he would have been securing her death.

Annabel, unaware of how close she had come to embracing death, walked through the now open doors and stared at the stairs that welcomed her. Like the doors they looked natural, flowing and immovable but she was mostly eager to see what awaited them at the top of the stairs. Needless to say, her first impression was disappointment. In the centre of the room was a glass desk with a single chair. The room itself was circular and huge, made almost entirely from what looked like polished steel, and around the entire edge subtle blue lighting reflected upwards against the metal walls. It felt very clinical and cold after the warmth of the oak but it still had the same subtle style that seemed to lay in the wake of wherever Sebastian passed.

"Do you like it?"

Not wanting to be rude or offend, Annabel just looked around smiling. "It's very…"

"…Cold?" He finished her sentence for her. Seeing the look on her face he smiled. "I quite agree with you, my office does lack charm in its present form but sometimes my work demands solitude and isolation in order to concentrate." He moved across the room towards the desk. "This is only necessary sometimes though." Sebastian waved his hand over a corner of the desk and a white light sprang from the glass near where it hovered. Immediately the room began to shift, almost soundless, as the walls dissolved to reveal they were merely shutters, receding to allow the glass behind prominence. By the time the transition had finished Sebastian could see the renewed awe in Annabel's face.

Chapter 17

As soon as he looked he knew he shouldn't have. The uneasy feeling he had felt in his stomach had been trying to tell him instinctively what logic would not.

Baxter sat looking at the logs. It had been done with such subtlety he had almost overlooked it. *Almost.* Who though would have the ability to access their internal logs *and* edit them. Even with inside help no-one except the highest level employees had access. He looked at the entry that had been modified, now almost impossible to show it was anything but what it now was. *Almost.* A system security breach would have made him uneasy at the best of times but this was not just some teenager with too much free time on their hands. It was not even a rival competitor trying to destabilise or discredit them. *Too precise. Too specific.* The stress of what to do was already showing physically. If he failed to report it and it came too light that he had seen it then he would have a lot too answer for, even if it did not come too light that he had seen it then questions may be asked as to why he missed it. Of course if he reported it as he felt he must… *What if it's something I would be better off not knowing about? Safer in ignorance?*

The breach unnerved him.

Baxter sat looking at it; the modified call log to Rotschlossen.

Chapter 18

Curiosity killed the cat. Mitchell Hale was disappointed at his final thought as unconsciousness claimed him. There had been no life flashing before his eyes, no regret, no sense of achievement and purpose. Only a moment of confusion, swiftly followed by realisation and panic, and now, nothing. Alex secured the makeshift noose to the surprisingly sturdy frame that held the shower curtain and waited several minutes to be sure the problem was resolved before moving back to the main room.

Carefully he removed the pictures lining the walls and the file from the bed, instead replacing them with the file that had been arranged by the company. The new file contained nothing of interest and the 'client' was fully briefed as to the contents and purpose. Hale's fingerprints were easily added to the documentation, his limp form swinging slightly as Alex released his arm from the gloved grip. He carefully combed the entire room for further signs of the case Hale had been working on but finding none proceeded with the final stages of the plan. Hale had paid for a few days in advance. In a place like this it was unlikely he would be found until his money ran out. *Not as if there's any room service.* Alex chuckled to himself and slipped the file inside a leather case contained within the rucksack he carried. He fastened the case and zipped shut the rucksack before preparing to make his exit. He looked at this watch. Still a few more minutes. He sat on the bed waiting, Hale's limp frame just visible behind the door. Alex returned to the bathroom and double checked to make sure there were no life signs. Satisfied there were not he checked his watch again. He stood behind the door and checked the passageway. It was time.

--

Steph pushed the button on the remote control. The igniters attached to the receivers flared to life and launched the rockets a second or so apart. The diversion was simple, but effective. The rockets were positioned on either side of the motel Hale was staying at. The rooms faced in two directions, fireworks had been placed on either side and if anybody should be looking in to the corridor or about to venture out, natural human curiosity would stop them. The explosions would also be blamed on reckless teenagers, the launching igniters designed to be bio-degradable so no sign of them to anyone that bothered to investigate and because of the time of year, the occasional random explosion and flash was virtually expected. The bangs came, separated slightly. Steph sat and waited.

--

Alex set off at the time he and Steph had specified. There had been nobody in the corridor and so no need to warn him off the diversion. The door closed as the first bang sounded and he set off on the second. He reached the ground floor without incident and was happy to see the fat man on reception had taken leave of his position completely. *Must have needed the toilet, I doubt Hiroshima would have shifted his arse let alone a few fireworks.* Alex chuckled to himself again as he slipped down a side passage and out of a service exit. He encountered no-one and entered the waiting car without incident.

"Problem resolved?"

"Target neutralised."

"Excellent."

They drove for a few minutes before Steph pulled the vehicle in to a side street and parked up to call the company. He confirmed the problem had been resolved and arranged for a vehicle change over, in turn he was informed the call logs had been suitably adjusted and that the go ahead for the final stage had been given.

"Well?"

"Job done."

"Good fuckin' job too."

Steph looked at the rucksack in the back seat and then turned to Alex. "So what was the documentation we're returning? Design blueprints? Insider trading info?" Steph laughed. Alex did not.

"Not our concern really is it." Alex shrugged.

"No, but you did see what this private dick was investigating."
Alex shifted uncomfortably. "Yeah."

"So what was so fucking important then?" Steph was completely focused on Alex now, why was he being so weird?

"Some runaway."

The blood drained from Steph's face. It all made sense, the look in that creepy Rotschlossen's eyes. Alex's behaviour. The extra money. "Was it Jamie?" It was more an accusation than a question.

"No Steph, of course it wasn't. Hey what are you fuckin' doin'?" It was too late. Steph had clambered in to the back and was yanking open the leather straps and clasps on the leather case that had been in the rucksack. He opened the file and stared at the face looking up at him. A stranger. A girl younger than Jamie, different completely. It wasn't her. Steph didn't know whether to be relieved or disappointed. "You happy now?"

Alex took the case from him, repacking it carefully and returning it to the rucksack. "Sorry mate. I was so sure though. That look in that mad sod's eyes."

"I agree it's weird that he would go to so much trouble to cover it up. I don't know perhaps it was some daughter of his or something trying to find him."

"I guess." Steph shrugged. 'Anyway. Fuck it. Job's nearly done so let's finish it and get a drink."

"Bit early in the day isn't it?" Alex laughed.

"Says the man who swaps milk for whisky on his cornflakes."

They laughed good naturedly as they drove to meet the other car. They changed at the safe house from civvies in to their suits and gave the keys to the driver that had met them, returning to the SLK, and then on, to complete their task. The handing over of the documents to Rotschlossen.

Chapter 19

The phone without a dialling tone glowed faintly. Karl answered it.

"Rotschlossen."

"I am calling on behalf of the City Waste Management Company Sir."

"Continue."

"The problem you wished to outsource has been resolved and two of our consultants shall be by shortly in order to deliver the waste you wished to dispose of personally."

"Very good."

The line clicked. Karl took a deep breath and sighed with relief. Things were starting to resolve themselves. Instead of continuing to worry himself unproductively he had decided to use the drive to discover why it was that the private detective had started trying to locate Sebastian's car in the first place. The answer had been surprisingly effortless to discover. After a quick search through the details Baxter had brought to him, Rotschlossen had discovered a website Christine's father had maintained concerning her running away and upon checking the email account that was linked to it discovered several emails had been sent back and forth between her father and an amateur photographer who had happened to snap a picture of Christine leaning in to Sebastian's car. The photographer's work was mediocre at best and very likely could not have believed his good fortune at finally having taken a picture that was worth something. The image was digital and had been deleted now it had served it's purpose and the only copy was now shortly to be hand delivered to him by the associates from The Company.

Perhaps this time his incompetence would not result in Sebastian's endangerment. Again he breathed a sigh of relief. There would be no further excursions he promised himself, no further endangerment of Sebastian or his reputation. *What of this girl though?* Ah yes, the homeless girl. He would just have to make absolutely certain nothing would happen to endanger Sebastian concerning that situation but for the moment there was little he could do directly... *Perhaps I should arrange for her to disappear...* First though the current situation is to be resolved. He sat back in his chair and waited for the return of Mr Harris and Mr Smith.

Chapter 20

Baxter paced around his office. He needed to make a decision and quickly. Logic would dictate he call Rotschlossen and tell him about it but his instinct said that Sebastian would be safer to go to. If he went to Sebastian though, over Rotty's head, then his mistrust would be obvious. If it proved to be that this was nothing or that they were both aware of it's existence then he would look silly and have made Rotschlossen his enemy. *Perhaps they were testing him.* It would explain a lot he supposed. The strange thing last night, all these vague discrepancies that he almost overlooked. *Perhaps they are testing me to consider me for promotion?* It seemed possible and would probably explain why Rotschlossen was so quick to get there last night. *I wonder if they are testing anyone else?* He stopped pacing and poked his head out of his door, looking to the office opposite where Cogburn was working. He seemed to be glazed over in the usual way when searching data for vague correlations. Cogburn looked up and smiled at Baxter, he waved and returned to his office. He sat down at his desk and dialled the extension to Rotschlossen's office.

"Rotschlossen."

He sounded strangely content. Perhaps he lacked faith in his abilities, hence his attitude last night and because of the time it had taken for him to respond to this one he thought he had proved his lack of faith to be justified. *Well I can soon change that opinion!* "Hello Sir. It's Andrew Baxter."

"Yes Andrew? How may I help?"

Baxter smiled smugly. "I have noticed something I thought you might wish to have brought to your attention."

"You've discovered something new?"

Baxter was happy to hear the new alertness in his voice. "Yes Sir. Would you like me to explain by phone or in person?" There was a silence as Rotschlossen made his decision.

"I have an appointment I must attend very shortly therefore I shall

come to your office once my meeting is complete."

Rotschlossen sounded agitated, which reinforced Baxter's belief it had been a test. A test Rotty was convinced he would fail but one he had instead passed. "Very good Sir." He replaced the handset and smiled smugly to himself. He returned to analysing the discrepancy. It had been done extremely well. Very professionally. Externally too he was amazed to note. *Only Rotschlossen or Sebastian could have authorised that.* He was certain that breaching the system security was, although not impossible, highly *improbable. No system is invulnerable but few come as close to it as this one.* Who would they trust to do it though? Giving somebody, *anybody*, the access required to modify Rotschlossen's call logs externally would require a huge amount of trust. *Sebastian was late in to work today though so perhaps he did it himself,* he hypothesised. Certainly it was a possibility. Andrew Baxter was given very high level clearance in order to be able to effectively do his job but even he did not have the ability to modify certain data and that was from inside.

He started typing up his report and printing out data in preparation for the meeting with Rotschlossen. Once complete he sat leafing through what he had compiled. There were very few positions he could be promoted too and the thought that he was going to rise further was a highly satisfying feeling. To be tested in the first place must have meant Sebastian had conviction in his abilities even if Rotschlossen did not.

He leaned back in his chair and smiled contentedly, waiting for Rotschlossen's arrival.

Chapter 21

The view was amazing and Annabel stood in total awe. The walls had moved away and in their place was seamless glass. It gave the impression that the ceiling was suspended magically above the floor as she could see no pillars of support. It was architecturally astounding, even to somebody such as Annabel who had no real knowledge of architecture.

Beyond that was the view. The buildings she had noticed when she had entered were taller than this one but had not been as intimidating or have as much presence as it did. From here she could see that there were only two buildings taller and both were equal in height. They stood like guardians, flanking the building protectively and the rest of the city lay at their feet. Sunlight would always fill the room as there was no obstruction to block it and in turn nothing to block the view of the city. She had never seen anything so beautiful, it felt like she was in heaven looking down on the world. The beauty of the mornings view had left her with an uncomfortable feeling in the pit of her stomach but the view from here was something else entirely. It melted her heart and captivated every aspect of her. The dark side of the city was completely invisible under the breathtaking splendour before her. Annabel wept. She felt ashamed to do so but powerless to stop the flow, held, spellbound by the sight before her. Sebastian's voice broke through the enthralment.

"Enchanting is it not?" His voice was soft and reverent, purposefully so for such was the view that anything less would have been blasphemous. Sebastian smiled warmly at Annabel as she forced herself to turn from the view and look upon him, cheeks glistening softly. He watched as she tried to speak and saw as Annabel's voice failed her, looking past him to the view behind him. He waved his hand over the panel again and the windows instantly became tinted to obscure the brilliance, not entirely but enough to diminish its hold on Annabel.

She looked up at him again as if wounded by the sudden removal of her source of pleasure, blushing slightly as she realised how silly she must seem.

"Do not be embarrassed Annabel. I too look upon the view with a feeling of elation but to live on elation alone would be a dangerous decision."

"I'm surprised you get anything done being able to see that out of the window."

Annabel stated this with such passion that Sebastian laughed at the conviction in her voice. "Yes. I have often wondered as such myself."

She watched as he sat down on the chair and removed a small box no bigger than a cigarette lighter from the inside pocket of his jacket and pushed it in to the desk top. A picture hovered suddenly above the desk and Annabel stared with renewed wonder. She could see Sebastian through the picture, sat in the chair the other side but only very slightly. He appeared to be tapping the desk like a keyboard and as she moved around the screen to his side she saw that a keyboard had appeared on the previously completely flawless glass. As Sebastian touched the desktop lightly, the 'key' would change colour slightly before returning to it's clear state with just a character designating its use. The screen and keyboard evaporated as quickly as they appeared and Sebastian smiled at her again, removing the small object he had pushed in to the desktop as he stood up. She realised that they were leaving. "Must we go?" She looked back hopefully at the now darkened windows and saw that the steel shutters were sliding almost silently back in to place.

"Yes. For now we must leave here but I promise we shall return here so you may see the view again, although it shall not be the same view. Every day little subtleties make the scene different, ever changing. No force can stand in the way of the progress of the city and of the life contained within it."

He made his way to the top of the stairs and reluctantly Annabel followed. She felt a little empty leaving the view behind but once she had done so and they were outside the doors she felt the spell subside slightly. "What was it you were doing at the desk?" She asked inquisitively, finding something new to distract her lingering thoughts.

"I was merely collecting some information I required from my computer."

"Isn't it connected to the other computers in the building then?"

"No. The computer terminal you just saw me use is completely isolated from the rest of the building and the rest of the company network. It is also isolated from the rest of the world so to speak as there are no means of connecting to it externally. All connections are made internally and can only be done so by me."

Annabel thought about this as they travelled downwards in the lift, leaving the narrow corridor behind. "Wouldn't they just need that box thing you used to start it up?" Sebastian smiled broadly as if she had said something extremely funny and Annabel suddenly felt very silly again.

"Please, do not be embarrassed. I would never be able to sleep at night if the security on my personal terminal were as lax as that." He stepped forwards on to a new corridor as the doors opened; he motioned for her to follow quickly and continued explaining. "The box you saw me use is merely a storage device. The computer screen activated itself when it realised that it's use was required but only once it confirmed my identity of course."

"Wait how would a computer 'realise' something? Don't you mean security or something? And how did it confirm it was you when you didn't put in passwords or anything?" Annabel had not used computers since school but was pretty sure what Sebastian was saying wasn't quite normal. He merely flashed a smile at her and winked mischievously. She looked down at the thick white carpeting, relieved Sebastian had supplied her with some clean shoes instead of the dirty old ones she was wearing last night. *Was it really last night?* They passed a large oak door, so prominent she felt slightly intimidated as most did when they passed by it, or worse, were called to wait to enter.

They continued to another oak door, similar in appearance to the one they had left behind but somehow not as foreboding. Sebastian grasped the door handle firmly and a soft click sounded, he turned it and pushed open the door. The familiar décor she had now come to associate with Sebastian was visible behind, although this time it seemed to have further little touches, such as bright art work and plush seating.

"This is the office I use to accommodate our most important clients and where I work when I am not upstairs." Sebastian walked in to the office holding the door open and gesturing that Annabel should enter. He allowed it to close as she walked forward and stood awkwardly in the middle of the room. "Please be seated." Sebastian watched as Annabel chose a comfortable fur lined chair and choosing to seat himself in a chair perpendicular to it. He sat thoughtfully considering what to do now Annabel was here, there was work that needed to be completed, albeit nothing overtly intricate or consuming but nevertheless had to be done. *Maybe I should ask Karl to temporarily accommodate her?* He asked the question to himself, chuckling inwardly as he thought how Karl would re-act. Karl would of course do as Sebastian wished but his eyes would betray his true sentiments regarding chaperoning Annabel in his absence. Sebastian considered a few further options before deciding it to be the only realistic alternative available to him. He reached for the telephone on his desk.

"If you will forgive me, as I explained previously I am required to complete some work today and as much as I may wish for you to accompany me while I do, unfortunately my patrons may not regard you as a welcome attendee of our meetings." He dialled a number on the keypad. "Therefore I shall ask Karl to accommodate you in my absence. Do not be concerned, you have already met Karl as he was the man who drove us to my apartment last night. Do you remember?" He watched as Annabel nodded but uncertainly. "Then it is decided." Sebastian sat waiting as the call connected and was surprised and a little bemused to hear connection diverted. *Karl did not have any appointments of which I was aware today.* He pondered what could have arisen to be important enough to command Karl's attention. If it were simply a case of a meeting with a colleague he would normally still receive calls to his office phone.

"Good morning. Mr Rotschlossen's office."

"Good morning to you Amanda."

"Oh! Good morning Sebastian, glad to know you are in the office. I was a little worried when you arrived late."

"You should know not to concern yourself Amanda. If there was anything wrong Karl would have notified you all. Speaking of which, is Karl not in his office?"

"He is Sir but he is currently in an appointment with Mr Harris and Mr Smith."

"Are you aware of which company they are visiting from as they are not names that I immediately recognise?"

"Unfortunately I do not. Sorry Sebastian. Mr Rotschlossen expected them though."

"Never mind I may have to interrupt if that is the case. Thank you Amanda."

"You're welcome Sir. Was there anything further I could help you with Sebastian?"

Sebastian heard the slight, if unintended, emphasis on the word 'anything' but chose to ignore it. "I require nothing further at present thank you Amanda." He replaced the handset and sat bemusedly wondering who Karl's visitors may be. He concluded that the only way to find out for certain would be to investigate in person and he stood, heading towards the door.

Chapter 22

"The documents as requested." Steph handed the leather document case to Rotschlossen, carefully watching his eyes as he did so.

"Thank you. Your work and the work of The Company has been greatly appreciated."

"The Company will expect the payment as agreed within 48 hours."

"The Company shall of course be paid immediately." Rotschlossen sat back in his chair, a weight having been lifted but the thought of Baxter's call was agitating him, restlessly darting in the recesses of his mind. *It is probably just further information concerning the private detective.* He decided it was not worth being concerned about until it proved to be a point of concern. Rotschlossen looked up carefully at the man stood over him. The familiar blue eyes looking at him with that same defiance he had seen before. *Enough.* He cast the thoughts from his mind so as not to betray himself but the glimmer of suspicion in 'Mr Smith's' eyes was enough to convince Karl he had not been quick enough to disguise his thoughts. "I am afraid I must now say goodbye to you gentlemen as I have much work to complete."

Steph looked at him, his face impassive, his eyes searching for further signs to arouse his suspicion. "The Company would like to thank you for your time and hope you have been pleased with the services as provided." Steph nodded curtly and stood with Alex.

"Very much so. Thank you, we are very grateful. Please allow me to escort you to the door."

Chapter 23

"Erm... Sebastian. Should I stay here?"

He looked back and saw Annabel sat with an awkward expression upon her face. Somehow he had completely forgotten about her presence in his haste to get to Karl's office. Berating himself for his absent mindedness and for his lack of courtesy, he bowed slightly in apology. "If you would be so kind as to wait here for the moment please Annabel as I am uncertain as to whom Karl is currently meeting with. It will be boorish enough for me to impose my presence upon them, to do so with your accompaniment more so." He smiled in response to her accepting nod and opened the door, stepping out in to the corridor, heading back in the direction of the oak door. He stopped before it and extended his arm to knock just as it opened.

"Thank you for your help once again gentlemen." Karl turned to see Sebastian stood in the doorway. "Sebastian. You are here. I thought you had been delayed."

"I was but I am here now." Something about Karl's behaviour intrigued him. "I see that we have guests. We have not been formally introduced. I am Sebastian and you gentlemen are?" Once again he extended his arm, this time with an outstretched hand of greeting. Karl moved to block him and allow them passage to exit.

"These gentlemen are... just leaving Sebastian." Karl shifted uncomfortably. "I shall explain very shortly."

"Indeed you shall." Sebastian watched intently as the men left Karl's office. Although professionally dressed, they had the gait of people trained to move in such a way. Of soldiers. "Good day to you gentlemen."

"Goodbye Mr Rotschlossen." Steph spoke with formality. "And to you Sir. Maybe we will meet another time." He felt Alex nudge him gently in the back and smiled.

"Erm... Excuse me." The frail hesitant voice was a stark contrast to the bold personalities present, causing all four men to turn in the direction of the interruption. "Sorry Sebastian, I know I said I would wait."

"That is quite alright Annabel, had you not followed I would have been required to return to fetch you."

Karl suddenly felt extremely uncomfortable. First Sebastian arrives at the worst possible moment and a few moments later it materializes that he has brought *her* with him. "As I was saying gentlemen. Good day to you both." He watched as they nodded and turned to leave but the girl stepped in front of them to block their way.

Annabel looked about her helplessly. "Sorry." She apologised to the men but did not move, she turned to Sebastian and apologised again, trying to find the words to explain herself. "It's just. Sorry. Can I... May I... ask you a question."

Steph looked at her with raised eyebrows. This girl for all her subtle designer clothing was very much out of place within this building, especially on this floor but of this Sebastian had seemed accepting enough, even if Rotschlossen had not. He did not see how a question could hurt. "Go ahead." He felt Alex's touch on his arm.

"We would be smart not to out stay our welcome *Mr Smith*."

"Let the girl ask her question." He flashed Alex a smile. "Mr *Harris*." Alex's cheeks tinged slightly but his face remained as impassive as Steph's had when confronting Rotschlossen a few minutes before.

"Sorry." Annabel could not stop apologising. "It's just... When I came out... I was looking for Sebastian." What she was about to say sounded ridiculous to her own mind, Sebastian would probably have her escorted to the closest mental asylum but she had to know. "I." She stopped to form the words properly and strengthen herself to say them. "I think I recognise you."

Steph's eyebrows raised a little higher, he was certain he had not met this girl before but he could see a vague familiarity in her eyes, similar to the look he had seen in Rotschlossen's. He looked at Sebastian but saw nothing but a look of uncertainty in his eyes.

"Do not be silly child. There is no way you could know this man." Karl snapped angrily at her and the look from Sebastian was enough to make him regret doing so. "I merely mean, how could she Sebastian?"

Sebastian looked resignedly at Annabel. "Would you please care to explain Annabel? How is that you believe you know this gentleman?"

"I might be wrong." *Please don't let me be wrong or I'll look so stupid.* "But, Mr Smith. Did you have a sister called Jamie?"

Chapter 24

There are certain moments in life that have a profound impact. Where every person stood at such an event is in such shock, numbness and silence quickly blankets the entire party. Such as the destruction of the towers in New York or the falling of the wall in Berlin, to those who understand the enormity of the situation it is paralyzing. To those who are not aware of the enormity, they are still affected by the reactions of those around them. To any who were to oversee the scene that followed Annabel's question, it would have been this role they would have taken.

Steph immediately paled, as did Alex. If their complexions would be described as pale, Rotschlossen's would be described as ashen. Annabel felt her heart stop as she realised the answer to her question and Sebastian stood waiting silently for one of them to respond.

Alex's first reaction was to look at Steph and brace himself to take any necessary action. He had of course been present when Steph had clobbered Riggsy and whether Steph liked it or not, they were still in the company of clients. Not only would an explosive reaction be bad for The Company's reputation it would be bad for both of their health.

Steph recovered quite quickly from the question considering what it was. What he found difficult to respond to was the overwhelming number of questions that flooded his thoughts. *Focus.* He told himself but he could not, the emotion swamped him but he could not explain why. After all, this girl may have simply gone to school with Jamie and recognised him from a photo or something but he knew that was not true. *The eyes are the window to the soul.* The truth of her question burned brightly in her eyes.

The truth of her question also burned brightly through Rotschlossen, instantly paralyzing him in its unexpectedness. As soon as the girl had breathed the words he had known why the eyes of the man had been so familiar to him. *Jamie.* First it had been Christine and now Jamie. If this one knew them both, as she undoubtedly did, it would mean a virtually impregnable wall of trouble to ascend or circumvent. It had been sheer coincidence that Christine had known Jamie, for this one to know them both too was terrifying, furthermore if this man, more, this Company employee was her brother, the implications were not even worth considering. Would the company side with him or one of their employees? The probability that always returning to the same area would result in girls that had known each other had never occurred to him. *Or had it?* Perhaps it had but he had once again allowed his own incompetence to override his judgement. Karl's mind flooded itself with indecision, he was panicking and could not seem to stop himself although he maintained his composure outside he could see the inevitable once 'Mr Smith' realised that Christine had been a friend of Jamie's.

All eyes were rested on Annabel, all except Alex who flicked his eyes back and forth between her and Steph. Annabel felt she was expected to say something but did not know what. She began to question why she had asked in the first place, maybe out of general curiosity, surprise even? She could not be sure but deep down Annabel felt she had to ask. Not for her own sake but for Jamie's. She could not explain why but she felt that if Jamie had been able too she would have wanted to stand where she was now. As she looked at Steph she could see the remarkable likeness to the photo. He had looked older than he was in that because of his eyes and that had not changed. The pale blue eyes looked deep in to her as they had appeared to do from the photograph in Jamie's things.

Chapter 25

"Smile then lad." The photographer looked at the boy with pale blue eyes through the viewfinder of his camera but the smile was hardly forthcoming. Instead he held more of a firm resolve.

"That's the best you'll get from our Steph I'm afraid." John Hennessey whispered quietly to the photographer, who nodded and waved Steph on.

Relieved, Steph tramped off towards the dorms to be allocated his room. The others had already paired themselves up of course but he didn't care, as long as he didn't have to share with some muppet he would be happy enough.

"Looks to be you'll be sharin' wit' all yer' friends aye Steph?"

Keith Boyd sniggered with his little group of friends bringing Steph to a halt. Boyd was always poking at him when he got the chance but was always careful to do it with the support of his friends. "You want to be careful Boyd. Your friends won't be beside you up there if something should happen to your support rope." Boyd scowled at him but Steph held his stare as he walked past. *Fucking arse. Always thinking he's better than me.* Then again perhaps he was. He hadn't had to save all the money he could gather by working crap jobs to come on this trip.

His mummy and daddy would have financed that no doubt. He gave himself a mental shrug and shook off the pang of jealousy he felt. It turned out that there were an uneven number of people and he therefore was sharing with no-one else. He was hardly surprised, he even managed to convince himself he was relieved. He dropped his Bergen on the floor and unzipped it, carefully setting his clothes out in the closet, setting aside one set and the boots he was especially proud of, to change in to. He grabbed his towel and carefully locked and double checked the door before making his way to the showers. He knew the others would not be back and ready to shower yet, he could still hear them pissing around outside. He stripped down and placed his clothes on one of the benches before stepping in to the shower and turning it on full. He braced himself as the cold water stung his skin but he stood in its path unrelenting feeling it slowly warm and then heat his skin. He never got to shower at home and enjoyed the little luxury, in fact he rarely got to clean himself much at all at home since Todd had fucked up the bathroom. *One of his unfinished projects.* Steph sneered at the thought, thinking of the torn apart bathroom at home with little more than a working tap. Sounds from the entrance brought him back to his senses. *The rabble have finally organised themselves inside then.* He turned off the shower and stepped out, unhitching the towel from a hook on the wall and drying himself.

"Hey lads. Steph is having his annual wash!"

He ignored Jack Baker's sarcasm, keeping his back to him and his comments. He could hear him and someone else approaching 'stealthily' but he kept his back to them. At the last second he turned around and grabbed Baker's outstretched arm, twisting it harshly up his back, ignoring the towel as it dropped to the floor. Shaun O'Neill went to say something and Steph smiled inwardly at the sharp intake of breath he made as he saw Steph's well muscled hardened body. "What you staring at Shaun? You want a date or something?" Steph watched him try and steel his nerves.

"Look Steph, let Jack go. You're hurting him."

For the first time Steph looked down and realised Jack was shouting at him, he twisted slightly harder and the shouts became whimpers for mercy. "And what would you two have done to me if I hadn't turned around?" He met Shaun's eyes coldly and looked beyond him to the group of others that were lingering at the door. Everyone was strangely frozen as if no-one was sure what to do, all the while Steph stood naked holding the whimpering Jack in the arm lock. A sudden call of *'Hennessey'* was enough to bring an end to that and Steph shoved Jack sprawling on the floor. As John Hennessey appeared at the door, Jack picked himself up and holding his arm gingerly, quickly slipped out with

Shaun on his heels.

"What's going on here Steph?"

Steph looked at Hennessey, then shrugged. He could feel no malevolence towards him. He tried to watch out for him when he could but he couldn't be everywhere all the time and what he did do was more than most of the other teachers. "Nothing."

"Nothing is happening or nothing you think I could help with?"

Steph turned and picked up the fallen towel, wrapping it around him again and picking up his bundle of clothes. "Nothing."

Hennessey shook his head slowly and moved his arm to block Steph as he went to walk past. "I can't do anything to help unless you tell me what's going on." Steph stopped and looked up at him. He stood like that, just looking deep in to his eyes, Hennessey could feel himself being weighed up by this boy but felt powerless to let him do otherwise. He saw a flicker as Steph reached his judgement.

"You're half right." He smiled sadly and stepped past Hennessey and back towards his room.

--

There was no rest that night, once they had settled their stuff in to their rooms they were called out to receive a demonstration of some of the climbing equipment they would be using. Steph was there 10 minutes before anyone else dressed in some of the clothes he had scrimped and saved for. The expensive boots still slightly shiny from their new-ness, comfortably fitting black combats and matching combat jacket. He felt comfortable and warm even with the biting cold, the fleece inlaid hat he wore doing much to keep in his body heat and similar gloves which he had been gifted to him from the guy he had worked for. He knew partially out of pity but he knew a large part of it had been out of respect for his determination at making the money he needed, so he had accepted them. As the wind cut a bit harder through the mountains, he was glad he had.

As the rest of the group slowly started turning up, he stifled a laugh. Kitted out in completely impractical 'designer' gear. Sports shoes, track bottoms and hoodies was the standard dress of most of them. Steph stood a little bit straighter, feeling even more snug and warm watching the discomfort of his unprepared associates. It was short lived though.

"Aye look at Steph. He tink's 'ees tryin' out fur the SAS."

"If you're an example of how the Chuckies prepare then I can see why our lads constantly stuff them." Steph notched a victory as he saw the anger well up in Boyd who's father was rumoured to have had connections to the Provisional IRA before they moved. Only Shaun flinched at the retort the meaning lost on everyone else.

The confrontation was dispelled by the appearance of Hennessey and two other men. One with short cropped hair and a hard look to his face, the other with bushy eyebrows and hair that would be better described as a mane. Silence slowly crept over the entire group as they strode forwards.

"Yer' dead later yer' fuckin' waster."

Steph did not have time to reply before the men were standing before them. Hennessey waited until he was sure he had everyone's attention before continuing and Steph noticed the two men accompanying him run a sceptical eye over the group in front of them, feeling a slight degree of pride as they raised their eyes appraisingly when they reached him but he was not sure why. Then he returned his concentration to Hennessey.

"...so remember to follow their instructions completely. Fraser." He turned to address the man with cropped hair and stepped back so the group would focus completely on him.

His voice cut with absolute control through the air. Some people need to raise their voice to be heard, some need to threaten in order to keep control. 'Fraser' had one of those voices that commanded immediate respect, this group of idiots and pretenders were not going to faze him for one moment. "Listen up." Everyone stood a little straighter. "This trip is about exploration. Not just of the terrain but also your physical and mental limits. Those of you who came expecting Butlins can fuck off home now because the rest of us are not going to compensate for your idleness for the rest of the fortnight. If one of us suffers, we all suffer." He ran an eye over the gathered group, as his gaze wandered past, Boyd whispered something to O'Neill and Baker causing them all to laugh quietly. Fraser's head snapped back, his gaze upon them, his voice level. "You three. Names."

He stood waiting.

"Well, ma' name is…" Boyd began but was cut short.

"Did I ask for an explanation?"

Boyd looked at him stupidly for a minute. "What?"

Fraser strode over to stand less than a foot in front of him. "I assume you meant to say pardon Sir?" The same level voice.

Boyd shifted uncomfortably. "Pardon Sir?"

"I asked you for your names. Not for an explanation. Now spit it out."

"B…Boyd."

"And you two?"

"Baker."

"O'Neill."

Satisfied, Fraser turned to address the rest of the group. "For the next two weeks we'll be doing lots of things that are hard and dangerous. O'Neill, Baker and B…B…Boyd here are the ones I believe are most likely to cause problems to the rest of us as they are too stupid too care about anyone except themselves. Remember, if one of us suffers…"

"We all suffer." Everyone chorused if without much enthusiasm.

Steph watched with amusement as they all went red, Boyd nearly scarlet as Fraser mimicked his stuttering response.

"Before any of that though, introductions. I am Fraser and this is my friend Cirrus, he likes to watch these exercises occasionally and is an old friend of mine with a huge wealth of experience. If you have any questions or require any help then ask either one of us. Questions?" He looked around again at the assembly and was met by silence, he was about to continue when he saw a raised hand out of the corner of his eye. *Ah it's him.* He looked over at Cirrus and saw that he too had noticed the raised hand. "Yes. You in the black."

"Steph Sir."

"Steph. You have a question?"

"When do we start Sir?"

Fraser smiled. "Enthusiasm. Hopefully the rest of you also have some of the same." He looked back to the crowd as a whole. "Well as I am sure you're all aware we were supposed to start right now. This evening. Getting to grips with the equipment and maybe even some basic climb techniques." The crowd started talking excitedly." But." He emphasised the word bringing them back to silence. "As you all decided to turn up dressed as if you were going to visit a shopping centre you can return to the mess and grab a meal and then I recommend some sleep as we'll be starting early tomorrow and when we do you'll be better dressed I hope."

A disappointed sigh escaped some of them but none of them sounded or looked as disheartened as Steph felt. They were already ruining it all. He had come here wanting to make the most of this and the first day was already wasted. He looked up and saw that the group were well on their way towards the mess so he lackadaisically began traipsing after them.

"Steph."

Fraser's voice stopped him. "Sir?" He stood straight as he spoke, making sure his feelings were kept inside, something he was well practised in, and made sure he addressed Fraser with respect.

"Where do you think you're going?"

"To the mess."

"The mess is where your schoolmates who dressed like they were visiting a shopping centre are going. Do you normally dress like that when you visit a shopping centre?"

"They're not my mates and no Sir, I do not dress like this to visit a shopping centre."

"Then you'll eat with us later. Unless you want to join them."

He did not need a second invite. "Not at all Sir. What do we do before we eat?"

Fraser smiled. "That depends how quickly you learn. Good choice of boots too."

Years of teasing made Steph immediately doubt the sincerity of that comment and he flushed with embarrassment. Fraser smiled and lifted his own trousers to reveal a matching brand and style. Steph continued flushing but now with pride instead. "Now Steph let's show you the Magellan."

--

Returning to his room Steph felt more fulfilled than he could ever remember being. He had learnt a lot in the past few hours and although they had spoken little, he believed Cirrus and Fraser had been impressed with how quickly he had picked things up. They had eaten dried rations but he had not cared as it had enabled them to spend more time learning things. He was surprised, although he could not decide why, when he returned to the rooms to find everyone still awake and making a racket. *They'll regret it in the morning.* He thought to himself as he grabbed a fresh towel from his room and dumped his clothes on the floor, deciding a shower was in order before bed. Upon his return he locked the door and collapsed heavily on to the bed finding the kind of sleep that is only possible after some healthy exercise.

--

Steph woke his eyes on the ceiling. It was early. He could smell the dampness on the air, he knew the others would find it difficult to be up when they would be expected and he smiled to himself.

--

The next few days were hard but possibly for all the right reasons. The group began to work more as a team, they even began including Steph as some started to realise he was by far the strongest performer among them and made their tasks easier. When they were split in to small teams of four Steph was quick to be chosen. Never one of the first, friends were chosen first but quickly that rule faded as those who performed better were picked quickly and friendships were relegated in favour of others, he was still down the pecking order but at least he wasn't last.

Boyd became increasingly annoyed, usually popular and quite good at sport generally, he found himself dropping further and further down the list in favour of other's as he continued to struggle and lacked the perseverance of some of the other members.

Generally though things were going well and the first evening became a distant memory to most as they improved and succeeded. Winning competitions and completing challenges. Fraser was happy with the progress and everyone else seemed happy too, after all this was what they had all paid to do. Abseiling, pot holing, orienteering, star navigation and basic survival techniques. Only the tip of the iceberg but flavour enough that they enjoyed the taste.

Steph should have known it would come to an end. Richard Clark was designated team leader and had already picked two of the strongest other members of the team. He received some resigned looks from a few of his friends but he just shrugged. The teams were to be quite big as there were only two, and they were to compete and it was clear Richard had decided to ignore all friendships and just build as strong a team as possible. Matthew Gable was the other team leader and it was his turn to choose. Unfortunately he had not had the same tactics as Richard and had started by choosing two of his best friends, who although far from rubbish, helped Richard's team look far stronger. They conversed quietly between themselves and a look on their faces showed they had decided to change tact, shrugging apologetically to their friend James, Matt called out his choice. "Steph, we'll have you next."

Steph had been sat against a rock waiting for most of the group to be picked first. Although he had moved up the choice order a bit, it had still been a case of, chosen before other's but only because they were terrible. He had never been chosen over the more popular members of the group. Until now.

"DAT'S FECKIN' STUPID!" Boyd exploded with rage and stormed off back towards the rooms. The group stood stunned looking after him until Hennessey started to give chase.

Fraser's voice sounded clearly. "Steph to Matt's team. Richard's choice."

--

Matt's team won. Just. The task had been assault and defend of a checkpoint. Each of them had been given a flag to be worn on their back. If the flag was taken then that team member was essentially 'dead'. The aim was to scale a rock face and then navigate across the countryside to locate the position of the flag. The rock face was defended by abseiling members from the defending team and the rest were camouflaged in the countryside to ambush those that made it to the top.

Richard's team were all captured before they caught the flag of the home base but were consoled by Fraser who explained the flag was very rarely, if ever captured and that his team had survived a very respectable time.

Matt's team were caught quite a bit quicker. With the exception of Steph and Matt himself, the initial weak choices giving Richard's team a noticeable edge. Most of Richard's team had been 'killed' but they were unsure of how many. They had navigated to the site of the base and could see the flag but they could also see two of Richard's team poorly camouflaged in the surrounding area, they could not beat Richard's time, they had to capture the flag. Matt went to move but Steph stopped him. "Wait." He whispered softly, his words barely audible above the wind. "We've missed two."

Matt stopped and squinted. He could only see the two poorly camouflaged members. "Are you sure?" He was uncertain.

Steph on the other hand was positive. "One of them is over there to the left of where Clive is visible and the other one is in the middle of that one and whoever is hiding on the far right.

Matt squinted. Now Steph had mentioned it, he could see it was Clive hiding on the left but could see no-one behind him. In between him and the person on the right he thought he saw some movement but was unsure. He decided to trust Steph's judgement and lowered himself back to the ground. "Any ideas?"

Steph considered, not realising he was suddenly leader. "We won't both survive against all four of them. If I can circle to the back and capture one or two of the ones that are hidden it might draw out the others."

Matt nodded his assent and watched as Steph disappeared in to the grass and rocks. A few moments later he heard someone curse and then Clive and who he could now see was Alex broke cover and chased Steph. To the left of where Clive had been hiding a flagless Richard was stalking back towards the rock face but he waved amiably to Matt. He continued towards the flag and was just feet away when he felt a tug on his back. Justin, Richard's first choice had appeared out of the grass in the region of where Steph had mentioned and had pulled his flag. "Shit." Matt cursed harshly.

"Sorry mate. Bloody good effort though, you came much closer than we did." Justin smiled and started in the direction Steph had headed when Matt noticed something.

"Wait a sec Just. Where's your flag gone?"

Justin looked around bemusedly, expecting a trick but to his dismay found his flag gone. At this point Clive and Alex reappeared over the ridge with a triumphant Steph carrying a handful of flags. "He caught both of you!?" Justin exclaimed.

"I caught you too and you didn't notice mate." Steph jested. For a second he thought he had over stepped the new boundaries that had been forged but Justin's face creased in to a smile.

"Very fucking impressed mate."

Boyd was sat cold, miserable and bored on the steps to the entrance of the rooms. The cheering crowd with Matt and Steph on their shoulders did little to improve his temper, especially when he heard most of the cheers were for Steph.

"You should have been there Keith! Steph ambushed half of our team and won it for them! Caught Justin without him noticing!!"

Jack's enthusiasm soured Boyd's mood even further.

--

Fraser, Cirrus and Hennessey stood in the cold morning air, the sun having just broken the horizon. Before them stood the group, better dressed than the first evening but only barely, they had learnt their lesson but had not really come appropriately prepared. Fraser took a breath to begin and stopped, quickly scanning the crowd again. *Where's Steph?* He turned to Hennessey and asked him but he did not know either. *Of all the people I expect to be on time every day it's him...* His thought's were broken by a scattering of laughter which quickly became rapturous.

Steph was walking from the direction of the rooms but was wearing nothing more than his boxer shorts. His face was barely contained the pure rage that was obvious but it was no redder than the rest of his skin, whipped raw by the harsh wind and cold morning air.

"Steph what is the meaning of this?" Hennessey sputtered.

"Sorry for being late but my clothes appear to be missing Sir."

"Why on earth did you not wait in your room until I came to find you?"

"I did not want to miss anything Sir." His rage was the only thing keeping him warm and the cold was the only thing containing his rage. His feet were sore and cut from the sharp rocks protruding from the ground and his skin felt numb. His knuckles were white from his tightly clenched fists.

Then came a chilling sound. Fraser was laughing but not with humour. It was forced. More. It was threatening. The laughter died on the lips of most of the group, although Boyd continued to laugh, although uncertainly, maybe even nervously.

"On the first day we had introductions." His voice quelled the last of the laughter and silence prevailed. Steph stood to one side, forgotten. Shivering. "In those introductions I explained something about the commitment to the group." He continued, everyone's attention focused on his words. He looked among them. "If one suffers we all suffer." Nervous looks quickly spread over the faces of all present. "One of the group is suffering, therefore the whole group must suffer." Boyd made to intervene seeing what was coming. "What is it boy?"

Boyd continued uncertainly. "Sir... well, what yae men'twas. Dat."
"Out with it boy."
Boyd struggled, not used to being condescended too. "Ya' meant if we ware

lazy we all suffer."

Fraser opened his mouth with mock surprise and confusion. "Did I?" His face reasserted itself to its former imposing stare. Boyd had the sense to keep quiet.

Steph made to say something but a glance from Cirrus stopped it before anyone noticed. Fraser continued. "If one suffers!" He waited.

"We all suffer." The reply was barely a whisper.

"Everyone. Strip down to your underwear. Now." Hennessey immediately went to intervene but a warning look from Fraser silenced him, from speaking to the group as a whole anyway.

"Fraser. This is not a squadron of recruits these are…"

"…Are sadistic little shits who think they can bully another member of the group." He whispered back harshly, silencing Hennessey. He turned back to the group. "I am waiting gentlemen." With that he started removing his own clothes, Cirrus following him and tentatively even Hennessey.

Boyd chose the wrong time to find his spine again. "Feck this. Ahm goin' home ter me pa."

Fraser finished removing his shirt and beamed a smile at Boyd. "I have the keys to the entrance to your rooms, the mess and the offices. All are locked. If you want to go home then you'll be walking." He pointed behind Boyd to the horizon. "The closest town, and phone, is 24 miles in that direction. Goodbye." His eyes glinted coldly and Boyd relented, although unhappily, and began removing his clothes. "Remember, if one of us suffers we all suffer. If we can end the suffering of the one we can end the suffering of the group." Everyone was now standing in their boxer shorts. Hennessey looked uncomfortable but was used to the cold from years of cross country running, the rest of the group were not boding quite so well to the sudden exposure. Fraser and Cirrus stood straight as if it was a beaming summer's day. "The solution gentlemen is simple. If we find this man's clothes, we may use our own. Until that time, we run." With that he set off at a gentle jog and everyone began jogging behind, very reluctantly. It took less than ten minutes.

"S..s..sssir." Baker could barely form the words his lips were so cold. "I know where the clothes are."

Fraser stopped and looked at him with barely masked disgust, a stark reflection of the apprehension in Boyd's face. "Where?"

"B…back at the rooms."

He lifted his voice slightly. "Gather your clothes and return to the rooms. Do not put them back on until I say so."

Upon returning to the piles Fraser bent down to pick up his clothes and called Steph over, handing them to him. "You want me to carry your clothes Sir?" He had adjusted quite well to the cold but his feet ached from little cuts.

"No Steph. You started suffering before the rest of us so you can now stop." He said it loud enough for everyone to hear.

Steph pulled on the too big clothes but found the boots to be a comfortable fit. He was certainly more comfortable than everyone else as they proceeded back to the rooms.

--

Fraser and Steph stood looking down in to the bin at the clothes. They were dirty but they could be cleaned. The boots on the other hand had been destroyed. Steph felt stupid as he felt himself choked at the loss of his boots. When he thought about how much they had cost him, how hard he had worked to afford them, to afford this trip. *Why did I even fucking bother!* He looked up to see Fraser looking back at him. "The clothes can be cleaned." He smiled cheerily.

"But my boots!" It was not a question so much as an exasperated cry.

"If you wash your clothes now and then put them in the dryer they'll be ready by mid-morning." He continued smiling. "As for the boots, you're already wearing some." With that he turned and jogged towards his office and his own room in nothing more than his boxer shorts, leaving Steph gaping beside the bin.

--

That day was strange for Steph, he was isolated again but not because of the same reasons as before. People felt guilty for laughing at him this morning. Matt had tried to apologise but had lost the words. Instead no-one spoke much at all and they spent the day rallying to help him as much as possible, without trying to be too obvious or saying much. Everyone knew Boyd had been the one to do it but there was no proof. They blamed him for their punishment that morning and it was his turn to also feel ostracised by the group.

By the time they dragged themselves in to bed that night morale was low and Boyd had successfully achieved the complete opposite of what he had set out to do.

--

The final day came and the top performers, based on scoring from everyone in the group and the instructors, were chosen. Steph still did not have the popularity to score highest in the group but he was one of them. The rest were put in to a hat and each top performer had to choose a name from it. That pair would then have to navigate the most challenging caves in the area without support from the instructors. When Steph's turn to choose arrived, fate handed him a nasty surprise it seemed. He was to be paired with Boyd. He refused to let it daunt him though and he stood by the luck, or bad luck, of the draw. Boyd sneered at the result and was clearly not happy about it but no changes were allowed. He was determined to make it as difficult as possible for Steph.

They were deep and alone in the cave before he realised the choice had not been a chance happening.

Boyd was hanging on to the side of the slippery rock face as water flowed down it. Steph had already scaled the ledge to the top but was attached to Boyd and could not continue until he got to the top. He began to grow impatient when a hand finally appeared over the top. "About time." He sighed and reached to drag him up.

"Get the feck off me. I dun need yae feckin help." He slowly dragged himself up on to the ledge. "Yae realise when we get back. Them lot. They'll forget yae. It'll be loike befur we ever got 'ere. I'll make sure of it." He grinned smugly, not paying attention, and his foot slipped on the wet edge. Boyd went crashing on to the floor heavily, smacking his head sharply against a rock.

Steph jumped forward and grabbed him careful not to let him slip back over the edge and drag him over too. "Are you okay?"

"Of course I am yae feckin eegit." Boyd sat on the ledge, blood trickling down the side of his face.

Suddenly it was all clear. Boyd would never allow Steph to keep the connections he had made to other's in the group, he would do everything he could to destroy it. Everything he had done this week. He had the power to prevent that though.

Boyd never saw the rock hit him. Chances are he never even felt it. Steph drove it as hard as he could at his temple, a few inches from where the original impact had hit him. Boyd collapsed in a heap to the floor. He did not move. Steph panicked for a moment but calmed himself. Boyd had taken his life from him for years and just when he had almost got it back he was going to take it again. Kill or be killed. He found the rock Boyd had struck and positioned the rock he held about the right distance away to be consistent with Boyd's injuries. He checked for a pulse but found none, no breath either. He placed his emergency whistle to his lips and started blowing as hard as he could. Not moving as had been outlined to them should an accident *(murder)* like this occur. It was not long before Cirrus appeared shortly followed by

Fraser.

The rest was a bit of a blur for Steph. He could not remember much of anything after that point and fell in to a deep and sincere shock. Many took this to be as a result of witnessing such an unfortunate accident but Steph knew the truth.

The police questioned him and he told what was almost the truth. They questioned him no further. He sat in Fraser's office staring at the wall. The sounds of sirens and the flashing light's died away. Everyone else was gone, some with comforting words before they left but after the accident they were to be taken home to recover from their own shock.

"It's a strange feeling watching someone die."

Steph looked up to see Cirrus stood in the doorway. In the past fortnight it was the first time he had actually spoken. Steph nodded dully.

"Stranger still when it's as a result of your own hand."

Steph would have started had the words registered immediately, as they slowly sank in he maintained control of his emotions and his reactions, a slight flash in his eyes betrayed him to Cirrus though.

"You performed excellently this week Stephen."

Steph sat looking back at him wordlessly.

"You performed most excellently in the..." He stopped as if to find the right word. "Removal? Of your problem." He smiled and continued. "I was particularly impressed that you thought to position the rock you struck him with in the correct position."

A bead of cold sweat slipped down Steph's spine.

"Intuition, initiative and improvisation."

Steph sat waiting for the police to walk in.

"The one thing that betrayed you was the rigging of the draw."

Indecision washed over him. What should he do? Run? Stay? What was Cirrus getting to?

"Stephen. You are still young but have an enormous amount of potential. How would you like to come to work and train with me?"

He was dumbstruck but found himself nodding silently to this man he barely knew.

"Excellent. I shall have it arranged. Also you should know my real name is MacLeavey."

He extended his hand and embraced Steph's. The ancient sign of a pact made.

Chapter 26

"How did you know her?"

Steph spoke first, his voice sounding strange after the silence, or maybe it just sounded strange because it *was* strange. Rotschlossen was still stood to one side as stationary as a rock, but not stiller than the other's present. "I didn't, I just recognised you." She managed to get out before her breath caught in her throat.

"How?"

Another question. Was he angry? She could not be sure but his voice was unnerving. "From a photo, you were in some sort of army jacket with a bag on your back."

"Bergen." He said the word softly as his eyes fell to the floor.

"Sorry?"

At her question he called himself back to the now. "A Bergen, not a bag... Well it is. It's not important. It was taken just before I left home for... just before I left home."

Sebastian's presence suddenly dominated as he stepped forwards slightly. Annabelle started at his sudden movement but he smiled warmly at her as he did so. "It would appear that Mr Smith..." He looked Steph up and down slowly clearly not believing it was his real name. "...and yourself have some catching up to do. May I recommend you have an early lunch at the employee cafeteria 5 floors beneath us, the food there is quite excellent and complimentary to our guests of course. Unless you gentlemen have other business of course, or if Miss Annabelle would rather spend her time with Karl?"

At this point Amanda appeared. "Excuse me, Mr Rotschlossen Sir. Andrew Baxter has asked if you still intend to meet him at his office?"

"Well that decides it then. Karl you can go and see Andrew and

Annabel can talk to her new friends."

"We should be getting back."

"It can wait." Steph replied through gritted teeth, then to Sebastian. "I would be very grateful for any news your friend has on my sister Sir."

Annabel nodded uncertainly but Sebastian gave her a reassuring nod. "Should you need anything, or when your friends depart, please just inform security of your wishes. They can be found on every floor and will not hesitate to assist you should you need them." He smiled pleasantly to Alex and Steph but the underlying message of his statement was not lost on either of them. "I shall meet with you again shortly, until that time please allow me to assign you a personal aide." As he said this the elevator doors opened and a man in a black suit stepped from it. He had an ear piece in his ear and looked much like a secret service agent who had lost his sunglasses. "Ah, Josef. Please could you accompany my guests to the cafeteria, do not intrude but please be sure to assist Annabel with any requirements she may have. I bid you farewell." He nodded politely to Steph and Alex and turned to walk back down the corridor.

"The restaurant it is then." Steph turned towards the lift with Annabel at his side and Alex a step behind. Josef a few steps behind them all.

Rotschlossen stood looking about himself, first after Sebastian and then after Annabel and the Company employees. He had wanted to intervene but could think of nothing to say. Now she was with them, what would she say? More importantly what would be the repercussions. Enraged, he steeled his emotions within, stepped from his office and closed the door behind him. *First I shall see to Baxter.* He had to prioritise, decide what was required and accomplish each goal individually. Rotschlossen felt the urge to contact the Company and request an immediate call back of their 'representatives'. *Would that arouse suspicion though?* It was a possibility and at the moment taking such risks could only exacerbate the situation. Baxter first then.

Rotschlossen received more than his usual side glances and changes of direction as he journeyed towards Baxter's office. The usual cold solidarity that surrounded him and kept people at a distance had been replaced by an aura of energy. People he passed could not immediately place what was different about Rotschlossen's demeanour but that did not prevent them from instinctually knowing to stay out of his way.

Chapter 27

Annabel sipped at the coffee, looking nervously over the top of it at Mr Smith's intense grey blue eyes.

The silence was uncomfortable but the need for answers was greater than the need to escape the oppressive atmosphere. Steph remained motionless but so much so it accentuated the fidgeting movements of Alex.

Alex was worried. No. He was *very* worried. The Company would not be happy about this personal escapade in the middle of a client request. If they found out. *If? When they find out.* He tried not to let it show in his face but he knew that he was going to be in the shit as much as Steph when MacLeavey heard about this. If the situation needed cleaning up then Steph might have to... *Well let's not worry about that until it's something to worry about.*

"So how do you know Jamie?"

Annabel turned her gaze away from the eyes and formed the words that had been practised over and over in her head since she had spluttered the question in the hall. "I didn't exactly know her, just knew a friend of hers." He sat back in his chair an eyebrow raised slightly. "A friend of mine too." Her eyes closed momentarily at the twinge of pain that recollecting Christine always brought.

"So what made you think I had anything to do with Jamie?"

"She had a picture of you but younger. Wearing a big coat in the mountains." She looked back up at him. "But your eyes are the same."

Steph sat back in his chair and raised his eyebrows slightly. "Jamie had the same eyes. If you had met her you would have noticed hers too." He braced himself for the question he had to ask. "Do you know where I can find her?" Annabel bit softly on her bottom lip. "What about this friend of yours?" She looked down. Steph looked at Alex, who shrugged and nodded towards the exit. Steph knew he was right but he couldn't allow this chance, maybe his only chance to escape him. "Well what *can* you tell me?"

"Not a lot I'm afraid."

Chapter 28

Sebastian strode back towards his office. Annabel was now out of his way temporarily, with strangers yes but within his building, so safe nonetheless. He thought momentarily about the situation. Karl's agitation. Mr Smith's reaction to Annabel. Annabel's recognition of him. Mr Smith's counterpart, Mr Harris' stance. Karl's apprehensiveness. He had acknowledged the entire situation in an instant. Faces. Expressions. Emotion, and of course, most importantly, the emotions they had tried to hide. The only person present who had been completely open had been Annabel. *Fascinating.*

He entered his office and buzzed for the first of his clients to be shown through, seating himself comfortably and storing his thoughts for later analysis.

--

Rotschlossen exploded in to, rather than entered, the area where Baxter's office was located. A junior assistant, Matthews, jumped, spilling the cup of water he had just filled from the water cooler. He looked up, glaring at whoever had entered so rudely, immediately changing his expression and backing against the wall as he met Rotschlossen's own icy scowl. Matthew's tripped over his own feet in his eagerness to rush back to his office, preventing his fall by slamming in to a wall before quickly rushing away down the corridor.

Spineless idiot. Nevertheless, Rotschlossen stood stationary for a moment, centring himself and calming for the meeting with Baxter. He walked calmly down the corridor towards Baxter's office and as he reached for the door handle, annoyingly, Baxter opened it from within.

"I thought you were coming sooner than that… Sir." He added the last as an afterthought, stepping aside to allow Rotschlossen entry.

"You have something to show me?"

Baxter eyed Rotschlossen carefully, unable to tell if he was angry or happy.

Well as close to happy as Rotty came. "Here you go Sir." Baxter handed over the report he had printed out, pulling out his chair for Rotschlossen to sit down. He watched as Rotschlossen slowly read through his report, becoming more and more unnerved as Rotschlossen's expression appeared to glaze over. *Perhaps he has missed the relevance.*

"The point of this is?" Rotschlossen looked up at Baxter coldly, carrying the air of someone completely disinterested in what he had just read.

Baxter was flabbergasted. "*Sir!*" He exclaimed, losing the words as his voice left him. Rotschlossen was not stupid, he must have seen what the figures meant. "The call logs. *Your* call logs." He leant over Rotschlossen, turning the pages of his report to the key evidence he had detected.

"What about them?"

"They have been *ALTERED...!*" Baxter stood up. "*EXTERNALLY!*"

Rotschlossen looked through the evidence before him. It was subtle, very subtle. Almost impossible to trace. *Almost.* Baxter was exceptionally skilled, even more so than perhaps he had given him credit for. Perhaps too skilled for his own good. He had not planned for Baxter to have detected this, he had to think of a plausible explanation but one did not present itself. He decided to kill two birds with one stone. *So to speak.* "Well Baxter, what do *you* think it is?" He said it knowingly because of course he did know but this way he would find out how much Baxter knew and whether it was too much.

"Well..." Baxter continued slowly. "I thought... It seemed to me that... Perhaps you were testing me... Us...? Me..."

"Which do you think?"

Baxter considered this for a moment. "Us. The department. It would be more productive to test us as a whole rather than just me individually. Also the information is available to at least three other people in this area." He conceded that maybe they had not been specifically testing him.

"And yet… It was only you that *did* detect it." Baxter perked up. *I was the only one that detected it.* He felt a glowing warmth of pride swell in his stomach. "If you would just satisfy my curiosity, for future reference."

"Yes Sir?"

"What gave it away as a test?"

"Sir?" Baxter looked at Rotschlossen. "Our company's computers are virtually impregnable, only Sebastian or yourself could have edited those files, or at least given clearance to do so."

"Very good Baxter. Very good." Rotschlossen actually smiled, much to Baxter's satisfaction he noticed. "Continue as you were but understand that this has not gone unnoticed."

"Thank you Sir."

Rotschlossen turned to leave before having a further consideration. "Could you remove the indicators that alerted you to the changes Baxter?"

Baxter thought hard. "At my current clearance I don't think so Sir. It would take you or Sebastian to do so I think."

"I shall temporarily grant you the access you require, email me the specific areas you need to access and I shall grant them to you… temporarily. I will supervise how you treat your new found clearances and determine if you can be trusted with them."

"Of course Sir. I shall re-instate the logs completely, you will not be able to tell anyone had ever tried to change them…"

"*NO!*" Rotschlossen watched Baxter cringe. "I apologise, you misunderstand me. I wish for you to leave the logs as they are but remove any indications that they have been edited. The original logs are inconsequential hence them being used, so the final part of your test is to see if you can remove the indicators that led you to it's discovery in the first place." He watched Baxter wrestle with this in his mind, trying to make sense of it. "If you do not think you can do it then I shall do it myself. It is of no consequence." Again Rotschlossen turned to leave.

"No Sir. Of course I can… I mean I would be honoured if you would allow me to prove my ability to you."

Rotschlossen smiled inwardly. "Very well. Email me as required." *That worked out better than expected.* Relief began to settle within him again. *Just the girl.* Yes, just the girl.

Chapter 29

Annabel finished her story. It was a much shorter version than the one she had told Sebastian the night before. She had hardly mentioned herself, concentrating more on her time with Christine and her stories about Jamie.

It certainly didn't sound good. Disappearing suddenly, her friend, this Christine, following. *She's really gone.* He heard the words inside his mind for the first time although they had been there for a long time. "She's gone." He looked at Annabel.

"They both are." Annabel felt tears building as she too finally admitted that Christine was not going to return. "I have some of her things." Steph's eyes returned from somewhere far away to refocus on Annabel's face. "I didn't want to leave them... to... I didn't want to leave them."

"May I have what you kept?"

"Yes, of course. I don't have it with me though, it's... Not here." Mr Harris leaned over to say something to Jamie's brother and he slowly nodded as if in agreement.

"That's okay. Thanks for... For telling me what you knew." He reached inside his jacket and pulled out a pen, he scribbled on to a napkin and handed it to Annabel. "I have to go but you can call me on that number and we can arrange to meet. I'd like to see the place you told me about and get the things Jamie left."

Annabel looked down at the number and folded it carefully in to a pocket. "Okay."

Alex and Steph stood up and Josef immediately started forwards to join the small company. "Is all well Miss Annabel?"

"Yes thanks." Annabel smiled.

"It looks like you're in safe hands here Annabel, I look forward to hearing from you." Steph smiled and an uncomfortable silence followed as they could not decide whether to shake hands, hug, peck a cheek goodbye. In the end Steph settled for a reassuring pat on Annabel's shoulder before turning to walk away with Alex.

"I shall accompany you to a waiting area for Sebastian if that is okay with yourself Miss Annabel?"

"Yes that will be fine thank you." But as Josef led her in the direction of a lift her eyes lingered on the direction Jamie's brother had left.

--

The waiting room was very comfortable and Annabel settled down to read a magazine she found in one of the racks. She was halfway through a story about how a man had married his brother's ex-wife when Sebastian appeared. She started slightly at his unexpected and soundless appearance. "Are you reading anything interesting?"

"Wha… I mean sorry?" Sebastian gestured to the magazine still clutched in her hands. "Oh, no. Just some silly true story." She smiled. "So, what now?"

Sebastian looked thoughtful for a moment. "I understand you ate in the cafeteria with your new friends?" She nodded. "Shall we return to my apartment then? Or is there anything else you would like to do?" She thought for a moment and then shook her head. "Okay, shall we go then?" Annabel stood and joined Sebastian, as they left the building a car pulled up to meet them and Annabel was surprised to see the day was already darkening towards night before realising that of course it was only late afternoon, winter bringing the darkness early. It had been so long since she had been warm, she had forgotten which season it was.

As they sat in the car Annabel's eyes were drawn to the streets passing by outside and once again she felt a burning in her cheeks. *Traitor.* She saw in the shadows, more shadows, but moving as they struggled to stay warm, sheltering themselves in the alleyways, trying to avoid the biting wind.

"How did your meeting go with your new friends today?" Annabel looked away from the window. "I trust it went well?"

"Yes... Thank you."

"Mr Smith was Jamie's brother you said?"

"Yes." She watched Sebastian raise an eyebrow and rub his chin. "I said I would give him the few things of Jamie's I kept."

"Oh?"

"In my bag, if you can call it that, Jamie's things that I kept, I didn't want to leave them behind."

"I understand." Sebastian smiled reassuringly.

"He gave me his number, do you mind if I call him so he can come and get them tonight? If he's free too." Annabel looked at Sebastian. "It feels wrong to keep them now I know the rightful owner." She watched Sebastian. His deep penetrating gaze locking with her eyes. She could almost see his thoughts forming behind his eyes but somehow they evaded her, barely perceptible flickers that even at this distance she had difficulty detecting.

"Of course."

His response caught her off guard, his eyes having entranced her, she jumped slightly in spite of herself. Sebastian laughed good naturedly and she allowed herself a small giggle. Sebastian reached forward and pushed a button that activated a panel, revealing a phone. He duly handed it to Annabel.

Annabel fumbled in her pocket for the napkin, when she finally produced it from the bottom of her pocket the number was a little smudged and crumpled but still readable. She dialled it slowly, deliberately. It had been awhile since she had used a phone. She heard the phone dial and then ringing on the other end and then the sound of the phone being answered.

Chapter 30

Steph and Alex walked down the steps to their waiting car. The SLK gleaming in the soft light of late afternoon. Alex sped up and headed towards the drivers side. Steph stepped to the passenger side and climbed in.

They pulled away smoothly and disappeared in to the traffic. Just another car in the crowd of many. Steph lay back and closed his eyes. His mind should have been racing but somehow it was completely blank. He was angry at himself for not having a million thoughts rushing through every fibre of his mind. He was angry that there was only one. *She's gone.* A small part of him was still struggling somewhere with the possibility that she was still alive but he knew that the chance after what he had heard was so remote it was unlikely to hold any water and with that thought, the small part of him still struggling to stay afloat sank below the water it had failed to hold. He opened his eyes as the car came to halt, surprised they had arrived so quickly.

"That was very fucking dangerous Steph."

Steph realised they had not yet arrived and Alex had driven the car down a side street and parked in an area of abandoned buildings. "Alex…"

"Don't *fucking* Alex me Steph. If MacLeavey, wait, what the fuck do I mean if? IF? IF? FUCKING WHEN! WHEN MacLeavey finds out we are both in the shit. *Both* of us. Because of you!"

Steph held Alex's stare. "I had to know." Alex flung himself back in the chair.

"I know. I know you did. But at the client's place. Steph. Fuck you could get us killed."

Steph did not bother apologising. It would be wasted and would only make Alex more pissed off. "Well fuck it. We'd better get back and find out if we've still got jobs," Steph looked at Alex with a sly smile. "lives too I suppose." They both laughed killing the tension dead but a subtle string of nervousness prevailed at the edges of their laughter.

They took their time returning. Taking the time to venture out of the city to open the SLK up on some of the country roads. The Company would know but they did not mind. They preferred their employees had a good knowledge of the surrounding area and the ability to drive at high speeds when necessary. Upon their return a guard stepped over from the entrance and waved them through. To a casual observer, just an ordinary checkpoint but if they looked a little closer they might notice the quite inconspicuous sight of the Heckler and Koch MP5 hanging from the strap outside his jacket, or the very slight bulge from the Glock 9mm stashed under the jacket in a shoulder holster. It was also unlikely they would have noticed the camera's checking Steph and Alex's identity with top of the range facial recognition software, or the retinal scan the guard gave them both as he walked up to the car. Just in case, the car was subjected to a thermal scan as it entered, just to make sure nothing suspicious was visible. Needless to say, entering Company premises was not a matter of routine, even for the employees.

Alex drove to the underground car park, parking the SLK in its designated space, leaving the keys. They walked to the lift and were met by Audi. Neither Alex or Steph could remember his real name, or quite how he had acquired his nickname but it had something to do with a massive crash he was involved in that took a lot of covering up. Audi still had a slight limp from the accident and now kept to admin duties. *Poor sod.* Steph thought as they followed him to the lift. They would be taken to MacLeavey's office to debrief him before they were able to go about their business for the rest of the day.

Audi did not bother knocking, opening the door and showing them straight in to the office. The familiar mane was visible behind the desk.

MacLeavey nodded to Audi and he closed the door silently behind them. "Welcome back gentlemen." Alex and Steph glanced at each other out of the corner of their eyes. "Good work today. Quick, efficient and a thank you from the client. We've already received payment."

"Debrief Sir?"

"Continue."

"Alex entered the building through the main entrance, I arranged for a diversion to the front and side of the building and waited to activate it."

"After entering I proceeded up the stairs."

"Witnesses?"

"Three possibles. Male on reception, ID unlikely. Was preoccupied with the television. One male and one female on corridor leading to subject's room. ID again unlikely. Male businessman anxious not to make eye contact, female prostitute although appraising of my excellent physique, was quickly dragged away by said male." Steph sniggered slightly before Alex continued. "Entry gained on pretext of looking for somebody. Subject terminated at approximately 13:15 hours. Case files collected, new files distributed."

"At 13:37 hours I activated the diversion in the form of loud fireworks."

"I proceeded downstairs and out of the rear exit."

"Meeting me in operational car."

"Job done."

MacLeavey looked content with their quick debrief, a written report would be unnecessary, specific files on this kind of thing were not a very good idea. Records were kept of course, but the specifics were in absence, only serial numbers pertaining to relevant companies.

"Good work. Dismissed gentlemen."

Alex and Steph left, once outside a short and relieved glance was all that passed between them. It was enough to convey their thoughts and words were an avoidable danger.

--

Steph threw his phone and keys on his bedside table, then dropped on to his bed. He tried to place how he was feeling and found that not only could he not place his feelings, he could not be sure he was actually having any. When Higgsy had made that comment about Jamie he had felt angry, defensive even? Now though.

He swung his legs around and sat on the side of the bed, his head in his hands. *Perhaps I'm in shock?* He knew he wasn't though. He had simply accepted the truth long ago and now had it confirmed. Laying back down his thoughts turned to what things the girl, Annabel, might have of Jamie's. He doubted there would be much but it would be nice to have something of hers. Something of his own. With the exception of his bank balance he didn't really have much. He had not had much since he had come here and that hadn't really changed.

Chapter 31

"Yae murdrin' feckin eegit."

Steph awoke in a cold sweat, MacLeavey standing over him, as he always seemed to be when he woke. It had been two weeks since he had joined the school MacLeavey ran. Recruited was probably a more appropriate description he supposed but whatever he had been, with the exception of the nightmares, it was the best thing that had ever happened to him. He was glad to be away from everyone, even his family. *Well except Jamie.*

"More dreams Stephen?"

"Sir."

"They will stop soon enough." He passed Steph a glass of cold water. He drank some and lay back down. "It will be a hard day tomorrow so try to get some rest." MacLeavey left and Steph thought about the past two weeks.

The school was like nothing Steph had imagined. MacLeavey had said *'Welcome to the Hotel California'*. Steph had not understood what he had meant but he made a note to find out. The pupils had to do a collection of modules in order to fill their timetable, but it was up to them which subjects they chose to study. The subjects were not normal subjects either, although they carried their names. In his first history lesson at the school Steph had learnt about the origins of the SAS and their importance during the conflicts that the British Isles had officially, and unofficially, been involved in. They had watched the news footage from the Iranian embassy siege which everyone had found fascinating, especially the lecture that followed about the strategic planning and execution of the SAS mission. At the time it had seemed extremely normal and much like an ordinary lesson but when Steph thought about it later he thought it quite an unusual part of history to focus on. Everyone had at least one physical training module each day, in the past week Steph had scuba dived in the school pool, fired a sniper rifle on a firing range and abseiled down the 6 storey administration block. Next week he was doing a parachute jump. He thought on this as he tried to get back to sleep.

He was still a bit of a loner but found it far easier to make friends here as the other people, although of varying ages (which he also found strange), were more interested in everyone else individually rather than their background. Except for the nightmares he found himself reasonably content.

As time passed Steph found himself learning a plethora of new skills or improving his old skills beyond recognition. Knife sharpening, camouflage, scouting, orienteering, unarmed combat, weapons handling, parachuting, scuba diving, pyrotechnical skills, survival skills and his personal favourite – marksmanship.

The first time he held the Barratt he knew it was something he would cherish. He was taught how to maintain and zero the weapon in. How to disassemble and reassemble, clean and oil every component. The excitement he had felt when he had first lay down to fire the weapon quickly subsided. He had looked through the scope and immediately everything had dropped away. His breathing slowed. His concentration focused. He relaxed. The cross hairs found the target. He levelled. Steadied. Gently squeezing his finger on the trigger.

The sound generated was incredible but he barely noticed, the kick being taken by his shoulder and the weight of his body. He heard as if from a thousand miles away the adjustments he was required to make to the sights. He did so quickly. Efficiently. His second round was nearly perfect. His third was the same, without the nearly. Marksmanship quickly became a skill he was renowned for, especially when coupled with his ability to seemingly vanish completely in virtually any given environment. At the end of his first term he came in the top five in the school in the areas of marksmanship, camouflage, evasion techniques and unarmed combat. By the end of the year he was top in each of them and held the school record for marksmanship, although the name of the record holder was not recorded, the distance, accuracy and time taken for the three shots was recorded. Everyone in the school knew it was his result on the table and he felt proud that everyone knew.

One day at lunch he remembered what MacLeavey had said and made a point of asking one of the older pupils. Steph remembered the way the boy had chuckled and told him it was a song he should listen to sometime. Once again he made a note to but other things got in the way and it was several years later that he heard it and realised what MacLeavey had meant but by then the connotation was something he had already realised.

When he reached 16 the driving lessons began. An hour a day, every day. The basics were taught and learnt quickly, the extras took slightly longer. Before Steph was old enough to even legally hold a UK provisional licence he was able to control an array of cars at high speed. Expertly manoeuvre, chase, escape. Steph quickly added this new string to his bow of skills and with it he approached his engineering lessons with a renewed vigour, the ability to practically apply the theory inspiring him to take an interest in something he had otherwise felt reasonably indifferent about. The day after his seventeenth birthday he took, and passed, his driving test. The lessons became even more intense after this though. Off-roading, rally skills, any conceivable driving situation was covered.

Steph supposed he had always known it was training for something. All those strange lessons, increasingly unusual as he got older. Even though it seemed obvious in hindsight, when MacLeavey first came to him at eighteen and handed him the mission brief, he had been surprised at the content.

Chapter 32

Steph's eyes snapped open as the annoying sound of "Popcorn" screeched from his mobile. *Alex you prick.* He thought, shaking his head in annoyance. "Thebe" *It was the girl, Annabel.* "Yes, this is Steph. Meet you? Sure." He wrote down the address as she recited it to him over the phone. "Yes. I know it." *Nice place.* "I'll be there about seven."

He shuffled off of his bunk and walked to the shower. He stripped and threw his clothes in to the linen basket.

The jets of water from the shower hammered in to his body, a little too hot, the way Steph preferred it. The water ran down his body in rivulets, tracing the toned muscles of his body, running over the scar on the back of his leg.

--

"Good morning Stephen."

"Sir." Steph remained standing in MacLeavey's office, until his lion-maned mentor motioned to a chair.

"How are things Stephen?"

"Good, thank you Sir."

"Your tutors are very satisfied with your progress," A smile glinted in his eyes. "as am I." He rose and moved to the window, clasping his hands behind his back as he looked out. "Do you enjoy your studies?"

Steph thought before answering, wondering where this was leading. "Of course Sir. I am incredibly grateful for all I've been taught."

"Good, good." He turned back to face Steph and once again, sat down at the desk, clasping his hands in front of him. "I knew you had potential Stephen and you have excelled even what I thought you to be capable of. Now…" He paused, the smile returning to his eyes. "Now is the time to put your skills to a more practical application." He pushed forward a manila folder and indicated

144

Steph should take it. "Take it back to your room and return to me with a solution by this afternoon."

"Sir?"

"Read the contents and all shall become clear."

They both rose and shook hands. Steph left the office, eager to see the contents of the folder. Upon reaching his room he locked the door and sat down at his desk. He took out a notepad and a pencil, took a deep breath and then opened the folder. He had been set tasks like this before of course but only by his tutors, never by MacLeavey, until now.

The folder contained background information on the target, maps and an itinerary of next week's movements. Steph analysed the information carefully, writing possible solutions on the pad, refining them, discounting the ones that would not work. Finally he decided on two solutions, both giving the maximum possibility of the desired outcome. Elimination of the target.

--

Steph stepped out of the shower and grabbed the towel from the rail. He chuckled to himself as he thought about the nerves he had felt that day, returning to the office, knocking on MacLeavey's door.

--

"Enter."

Steph pushed open the door and entered MacLeavey's office with his notes and the folder in hand. MacLeavey gestured to the chair and Steph took a seat.

"You have a solution Stephen?"

He nodded. "Two."

"Two?" MacLeavey rubbed his chin. "Why two?"

"The first one is entirely dependent on the itinerary and route remaining the same, the second allows for a little more flexibility should anything change."

"Always good to have a plan b eh?"

"Exactly Sir."

Steph spent the next hour outlining first one plan, then the other to a silent MacLeavey. He then spent a further hour answering questions MacLeavey had about the plans and possible problems with them. MacLeavey sat back in his chair.

"You have done well Stephen. Now the real question. Do you feel confident that you can implement these plans successfully?"

"Sir?" *Was he asking him to actually carry this out?*

"School is over Stephen. It is time to see if you are as successful outside the classroom as within it. Are you ready?"

Steph suddenly felt strangely calm. His plan, designed around his strengths. If the intel he had been provided was accurate he was quietly confident. His eyes levelled and met MacLeavey's. "I'm ready."

--

Steph dressed and collected his phone and wallet from his bedside cabinet, as an afterthought he also tucked the Sig P229 Blackwater inside his jacket holster. He also decided to rectify Alex's change to 'Popcorn' to something a little more ambiguous. He opened the door and walked down the corridor, heading towards the lift that would take him back to the storage garage. Arriving at the bottom he was met by Audi.

"Off somewhere Steph?"

"Yes mate, anything will do."

"Very good, the blue RS4 in G is available."

"Thanks." Steph strolled across the lot to section G which mostly carried "normal" cars, although they had all been heavily modified to increase performance, handling, etc. He found the RS4, climbed in and started the engine, the keys of course sitting in the ignition waiting to be turned. As he pulled up the ramp and in to the cool night air his mind drifted back to the night of the first mission.

--

She strode across the room, pulling her dress over her head as she did so. Sitting on the edge of the bed she grabbed his trousers and pulled him towards her. She unzipped his trousers and pulled him free, teasing him with her tongue before taking him deep in to her mouth. He moaned, pushing his fingers in to her hair as he felt her warm lips working on him. He reached down, pushing his hand in to her bra and freeing her breast, massaging it roughly as she brought him to climax. He came heavily and she choked slightly as he pushed deep in to her throat. She quickly recovered swallowing most of what he gave but a little dribbled out of her mouth and down over her chin and breasts. Flicking her tongue out, she cleaned him and licked her lips, collecting up what had spilled on to her breasts with her fingers, she licked them clean too. He grinned down at her, pulling a small, clear, plastic bag from his jacket pocket. Laying a mirror flat he emptied some of the powder from the bag and cut it up with a card from his wallet, he sniffed the line in a well practiced fashion, leaving little residue behind. Handing her the mirror, she pushed back her hair and copied him, taking the line in one long sniff. Dabbing her nose she grinned and the both gasped as the effects hit them. Grinning, he wandered out in to the bathroom. She collapsed back on the bed, running her hands down her body, tingling from the sensation of the cocaine. Sitting up abruptly she skipped in to the bathroom too.

From his hidden vantage point in the closet, Steph waited until he was happy they were both away from the room. Strangely he was not nervous. The unexpected change to the itinerary reinforcing his confidence as he had planned sufficiently to have a back up plan. Had they discovered him in the closet, or if they discovered him as he left, it would make this situation a little more difficult than he had planned but he moved silently across the room. The bathroom door was only slightly ajar, and through the gap he could see him penetrating her from behind. *Good, that will keep them occupied for the moment.* He picked the plastic bag up from where it had been left, moving it to his inside pocket, at the same time removing an identical looking bag, with identical looking white powder. This he then placed in the position the other had been laying in before returning to his position in the closet. He heard a scream as she climaxed and a grunt as he again came. Their deep breathing resonating in the echoing environment of the bathroom. The room brightened as the bathroom door opened fully, her now completely naked, striding across the room, a little bit shaky on her legs. He followed, dropping to the bed. "How about a top up?" He winked and reached again for the bag and emptied a pile on to the mirror again. Splicing it in to two large lines, first he snorted his line before passing it to her to the same again. They both collapsed back on the bed, gasping from both the effects of the narcotic but also from the lingering effects of the sex. They both lay on the bed for a time and then he pulled himself up in to a sitting position. It was then that he realised something was wrong. He felt a blinding pain in the front of his skull and inside an aneurysm exploded causing a subarachnoid haemorrhage in his brain. Blinking tears from his eyes he looked over to her for help but the blood shot eyes and the blood leaking from her own nose reinforced the futility he felt. Blackness swamped him and he collapsed back on to the bed.

Steph waited a further 20 minutes before leaving the closet. He approached him, checking for a pulse, finding none, he moved to the other side of the bed to check for her pulse, even though her glassy gaze conveyed the knowledge already. He looked down at her. Pity. She was a very attractive girl. *All wars have their victims.* Checking for a pulse and finding none, he moved to the window he had used to gain entry. It was unlikely they would be discovered until the morning and, even when they were, the obviousness of the cause of death would be likely to prevent any retaliation attack and if an autopsy was performed, which considering the circumstances was very likely, the overdose would be confirmed. *Too much of a bad cut.* Reaching the ground he was careful to rest his foot on the edge of a large terracotta plant pot. It would not do to leave suspicious footprints in the soft mud. Reaching the road, staying to the shadows, his first mission complete, Steph made his way in to the darkness.

--

Luciato Riina. He had barely acknowledged the name at the time, concentrating on the more important details of security, routes, associates. The mission was a success. There were no repercussions. MacLeavey was happy. The death of the woman was unfortunate and strangely, it still bothered him. He never did find out her name, just some prostitute it seemed. No one cared. No one acknowledged her death.

As he drove he thought about Jamie. No one acknowledged her death either. He had given up trying to convince himself she was still alive. *Sometimes, even if you do not want to believe something, you know in your heart it's true.* Her words. She used to say them to him all the time when they were children. Before he had left. He felt responsible for her death and a deep gnawing in his stomach became more pronounced as he got closer to the address Annabel had given him. He wondered what possessions of Jamie's she had.

Chapter 33

Sebastian guided Annabel through the door and closed it behind him.

"Thank you for today."

Sebastian raised a questioning eyebrow. "Today?"

"For being so understanding. I mean the chances of running in to Jamie's brother, it's amazing."

"Ah yes. Mr Smith."

"Yes, Steph."

"And his friend, Mr Harris."

"Yes. I didn't catch his first name, he seemed a bit annoyed about me talking with Jamie's brother."

"Yes. They did seem a little on edge about it all."

"What were they doing for you?"

"For me?" Sebastian looked genuinely surprised. "I have no idea, which bothers me a little. I usually know everything that happens within my building. I must remember to ask Karl about it."

Annabel shuddered involuntarily at the mention of Karl Rotschlossen, something about him gave her the creeps despite Sebastian's endorsement of him.

"You had better shower. Shall I prepare dinner for your guest too?"

She felt suddenly embarrassed. "I'm sorry, I don't know. You don't mind him coming do you? I know I'm imposing."

Sebastian smiled warmly. "It is not a problem, really. I shall make some for him just in case. You can go wash up for dinner." He turned towards the kitchen.

"Sebastian." He stopped and turned back to her. "Thank you."

He smiled and turned back towards the kitchen. Feeling better she went to her room. *My room.* She sat on *her* bed and felt a sense of belonging, her gratitude to Sebastian overwhelming. Pulling out her bag containing some of Jamie's things she began sorting through the contents so she could give them to Steph when he arrived.

Chapter 34

Steph pulled up outside the building. He approached, the door being opened by *Paul*. He nodded in thanks. The doorman curtly returning his nod out of politeness. He approached the reception desk.

"Good evening Sir. How may I help?"

He explained who he was there to see and the man made a call to Sebastian. "Very good Sebastian." He hung up the phone and turned smiling to Steph. "I shall give you entry to the lift, if you give me your car keys I will have a valet park it for you. If you call down when you leave I shall have it brought around for you."

"Thank you."

He entered the lift and the man on reception pushed the button for the penthouse, walking away as the doors closed. Steph waited as the lift ascended to the top floor, the doors opening on to the corridor Annabel had seen for the first time the night before. He approached the door and rapped gently against it. The door opened and Sebastian smiled warmly. "Welcome, Mr Smith. Annabel will be out shortly." He closed the door behind him.

"Nice place you have."

"Thank you. I did not know if you would have eaten so I have made enough for you to join us for dinner if you wish."

"That's very kind of you. I'd appreciate that."

Sebastian lead the way to the dining room and gestured Steph towards a seat at the table. "Would you like a drink Mr Smith, maybe a glass of wine?"

"Please, call me Steph."

"Steph it is."

"Water will be fine thanks. I drove here."

"You do not drink at all when you drive?"

"Never."

"A very admirable quality." Sebastian nodded politely and entered the kitchen leaving Steph to look around the plush apartment. The views from the window were breath taking and he stood to look out.

"Your water."

"Thanks." He took the glass from Sebastian and sipped the ice cold water. "It's quite a view you have from up here."

"Yes, I like to have a good view of things."

Annabel walked in to the room dressed in fresh clothes. "Hello Steph." She smiled nervously and he nodded in greeting.

"Shall we eat?" Annabel and Steph sat at the table and Sebastian disappeared in to the kitchen, returning a few moments later with a large bowl of salad and carbonara. "Please help yourselves." Serving himself a large portion he passed the bowl to Annabel. "So, Steph. What was your business at my building today?"

Steph almost choked on the mouthful of food he had just started to eat, taking a sip of water he turned to Sebastian. "You mean Mr Rotschlossen did not inform you?"

Sebastian cocked his head to one side thoughtfully. "Not exactly, no."

"He had a problem he needed help with from the company I work for."

"And which company might that be may I ask?"

Steph looked uncomfortable. He lifted his head, levelling his gaze directly at Sebastian. "The Company."

A flicker of recognition registered briefly in Sebastian's eyes. "I was not aware we were outsourcing to The Company. I trust whatever the problem was, it was rectified?"

"Of course."

Annabel looked at each of them. "Am I missing something here?" She asked nervously, trying to sound light hearted.

"Nothing that you need to concern yourself with Annabel, we are merely discussing business. However I would be interested to know about this in a little more detail and so I must remember to ask Karl about it once we are done here."

An uncomfortable silence descended over the table and they finished eating under it. As the last of the food was eaten Sebastian rose and begun to clear away the dirty dishes, Steph and Annabel rose too and made to help but Sebastian stopped them. "Please, leave these to me. Why do you not both go and discuss what it is you need too, I need to call Karl about some things anyway." As he said this he looked at Steph. "I shall make some coffee too if you would both like some."

"That would be great, thanks." Steph accepted eagerly, grateful to be changing the subject away from 'work'.

"In that case I shall see you both shortly."

Chapter 35

Rotschlossen looked at the email from Baxter. Reading between the lines he could see Baxter congratulating himself on his own excellence. Rotschlossen decided to let it be as Baxter had indeed shown a great deal of skill in detecting what he did. He considered contacting the Company for a moment to complain about 'Mr Smith' but decided better of it. Things appeared to have remedied themselves, so better not to make waves unnecessarily.

He wandered across the room to look out of the window and in to the grounds, leaning on the big oak desk with the comfortable red leather chair to one side. Home now, he felt more at ease. Of course the main company building was more than secure but it was also full of people. Karl had always preferred a quieter existence. His mind drifted to the problem of the girl and her recognition of 'Mr Smith'. He of course had known in that instant why those eyes were so familiar but that was not of concern. There was no way of it all linking back to him. *No way to endanger Sebastian.* He closed his eyes against the thought. He must protect Sebastian from his mistakes, he trusted him to not make mistakes, he trusted him to protect him. Sebastian of course was oblivious. He had seen the expressions in the hall and would have undoubtedly picked up on them but he showed no sign that he had a deeper understanding of the potential problems afoot. *First the investigator and now this 'brother'.* Karl suddenly felt old. He sat down in the big leather chair feeling his concerns subside a little as he sank in to the soft cushioning. He sat staring out in to the night until the telephone beside him rang.

Chapter 36

"Here it is." Annabel closed the door and walked across to the bed where she had neatly laid out the contents of her bag that had belonged to Jamie. "It's not much I know but she would have wanted you to have it." She looked up at Steph who was standing uncomfortably by the door and beckoned him over. Steph sighed deeply and crossed the room. "Are you okay?"

He smiled humourlessly. "Yes. I... All these years I was convincing myself she was still alive."

"She might still be." Annabel smiled doubtfully.

"Sometimes, even if you do not want to believe something..."

"..., you know in your heart it's true." Annabel cut him off.

"Exactly. Where did you hear that? Jamie used to say it all the time when we were... When we were younger."

"Christine used to say it too, I guess she picked it up from Jamie."

"I guess." Steph started looking through the bits and pieces on the bed. Stopping when he got to a small wooden lion. He smiled. "I bought this for her. I went on a school trip to some zoo and found some money when we were walking around. I used it to buy her this." His eyes glazed slightly as his thoughts drifted back to that day. He had only been able to go on the trip as the contributions to attend were 'voluntary'. He placed it back on the bed gingerly, his eyes moving over the other bits and pieces. "Ah this photograph." He picked up the picture of him at the out of bounds trip. *Where it had all begun.* "I didn't see Jamie much after this was taken, maybe twice."

"What happened?"

"I was accepted to a school for... gifted children. It was free and I lived there until I was 18." Annabel nodded silently. Steph continued looking over the other oddments before his attention was drawn to the narrow strip of photographs, the kind you get from a booth for taking passport photographs.

There was Jamie, older than he remembered but with her, the other girl staring back at him. The pretty blonde face that until this morning he had not seen.

"That's Christine."

He looked at Annabel as she told him what he already knew. The girl in the picture was the same girl the private investigator had pictures of. His mind reeled, something was not right, his instincts were screaming at him. That creepy Rotschlossen's look of recognition, how anxious he had been, the oppressive atmosphere in the hallway when Annabel had appeared. They knew what had happened to Christine and suddenly, every fibre of his body told him, they knew what had happened to Jamie too.

Chapter 37

"Hello Karl." Sebastian sat comfortably on the plush couches in the lounge, the phone placed to his ear, a glass of red wine held casually in his right hand.

"Good evening Sebastian."

Sebastian smiled at the reassuringly strong voice of Karl. He had always been there for him, ever since he was a child. "The Company." He said nothing else, waiting for Karl's response.

"Sebastian... I... What do you mean?"

Sebastian took a sip of his wine, savouring the rich, deep spiciness of the 1961 Chateau Cos D'Estournel. "I mean, Mr Smith is here visiting Miss Annabel regarding some artefacts of his sister in which she is of possession and over dinner he mentioned he worked for The Company." Karl was silent on the other end of the phone. "I would like to know for what purpose we were outsourcing to the company."

"The matter is resolved Sebastian, it is nothing for you to be concerned with."

"On the contrary my dear friend, if I am unaware of the circumstances how am I able to decide whether or not I should be concerned?" He heard the door to Annabel's room open. "Karl, I must go, I will however be calling you again shortly for clarification." Sebastian pushed the button to hang up and turned to face Annabel and Steph.

Steph's face was ashen.

"I trust everything is okay?"

Steph brought his eyes up to Sebastian. He could feel the weight of the Sig pushing against his back and it took everything he had to resist drawing it and finding out exactly what this bastard knew. *Calm down.* He took a deep breath, Sebastian might not know anything he reasoned, he hadn't known about the company involvement, Rotschlossen had requested the help. *Rotschlossen.*

"Steph feels a bit ill." Annabel said worriedly.

"Yes." He said weakly, coughing slightly, clearing his throat. "Yes," He said again more strongly. "Thank you for your hospitality Sir."

"Please, call me Sebastian." He smiled offering his hand. "Would you like me to arrange transport for you? You can collect your car tomorrow."

"No. Thank you, but no. I'm sure I'll be fine it's just the emotion over my sister. Jamie." He put emphasis on her name, watching closely for a reaction, using all of the skills he had been taught. *Nothing.* He mentally sighed in relief at not having drawn the Sig on him.

"I can only imagine how you feel as I have no siblings myself. I hope whatever Annabel was able to give you aids you in finding her."

Steph nodded towards Sebastian in silent thanks. Inside his emotions were raging, he knew he needed to clear his mind. "Thank you for your hospitality tonight, and Annabel, thank you for Jamie's things. I'll see you both around." Dazedly he walked to the door, letting himself out, the door closed silently behind him.

Annabel felt a little upset. She hoped that his sister was ok but in Jamie's own words; *Sometimes, even if you do not want to believe something, you know in your heart it's true.* This seemed strangely relevant to the tragic events surrounding Jamie's life. She smiled weakly at Sebastian. "You have had an eventful day." She nodded wearily. "Would you like to shower before you go to bed?" Annabel nodded. She suddenly felt very lonely. She had a need to feel wanted, to feel loved. "I shall fetch you some fresh towels."

"Sebastian…"

"Yes Annabel?"

She began to feel her nerve slipping. "Would you like to join me?" As the words left her lips she felt her ears reddening. She forced herself to raise her eyes to Sebastian, he was smiling patiently. He stepped across the room towards her, although moving slowly he was there in front of her in an instant. She felt the wall at her back as she looked up with need in to his eyes. Locking her with his gaze, she gasped as she felt his hand gently touch her neck, sliding down the side of her breast, her tummy to rest on her hip. She could smell his sweet breath, inches from her face, she was desperate for him to kiss her, she could feel her excitement as her erect nipples strained against her top and she became moist. *Take me, please take me.* Her mind screamed with want, with passion, with lust.

Sebastian smiled. "You are a very attractive young lady Annabel." His voice was husky, deep, Annabel shivered with need. "However, it has been an unusual couple of days for you and I would prefer that should you decide this to be something you would want, the decision was made when your mind was clearer." He smiled and gently stroked her cheek. "I shall fetch you some towels." He turned and disappeared down the corridor.

Annabel collapsed back against the wall. She felt completely confused, exhilarated, rejected, wanted but unwanted. Her mind refused to settle on one emotion as it swam with thoughts. She padded to the bathroom dazedly removing her clothes as she went leaving them in a small trail not completely by accident. Once in the bathroom she looked at herself in the mirror again. She already looked so much healthier than she had yesterday evening but she was still a little gaunt. She turned the water on in the shower and climbed in, jumping slightly as the icy cold water from the pipes hit her before gradually warming to a comfortable temperature. Thoughts of Sebastian flashed through her mind, of his eyes, of his smile. The want she had felt in the lounge began building in her again as she gently massaged her body with the rich smelling soaps, closing her eyes. Her hands glided easily over her breasts, her nipples hard again and down, over her stomach. *Sebastian.* She could see him in her mind, feel him. As she touched herself she released a loud gasp of want and need, biting her lip to prevent the cries from escaping her lips. She continued slowly, unhurriedly, the way she thought Sebastian would touch her. She felt the warmth building, it had been so long since she had felt this, so long since she had been able to indulge herself in this way. As she felt the release a loud cry escaped her lips, unable to keep the grip on her lip. She pushed her fist in to her mouth to stifle the sound but waves of ecstasy rushing through her numbed the noise. She stood shakily in the shower. The hot water continuing to run over her body. Annabel felt a little dizzy, her legs felt unsteady. She reached out with an uncertain hand and turned off the water. Panting for breath, she opened the shower door and stepped out on to a crisp white towel that had been laid for her. Next to the sink were some more towels, carefully folded like the pile of the clothes beside them that she had discarded in the hall. She looked to the now closed door she had intentionally left open and sat heavily on the edge of the bath wondering if he had stayed to watch.

Chapter 38

Steph pulled the car in to the underground car park. A look of silent resolve in his eyes. He had work to do. Working for and being trained by the company had given him the skills necessary to get to the bottom of this and nothing was going to stand in his way. He silently thanked God that he had had sufficient hindsight to stash some money and things in case they were needed. He silently prayed they wouldn't be. As he walked towards the lift he thought of the strangeness of thanking and praying to a God he did not believe existed. The lift opened at the computer level. The security protocols should be enough to mask his searches from Rotschlossen's techies but he knew the Company would know everything he had looked at. *But if you're going to attack someone it's better to have an element of surprise.* Perhaps it wouldn't be picked up anyway, after all he had just done a job there today, it might go unnoticed as being associated. *Yeah and pigs might sprout wings and fly.* He knew the jokes he was telling himself were to keep him calm which in itself added to his nervousness. He took a deep breath and stepped in to the computer room.

--

MacLeavey stood with his back to Alex, his hands clasped loosely there as he finished. Waiting until he was sure there was no more MacLeavey returned to his seat and looked thoughtfully at Alex.

Alex was nervous. He had struggled with what to do ever since returning but it was his neck on the line too so fuck it. If Steph wants to rile the Company then let him, he wasn't taking Alex down with him. He had decided to debrief MacLeavey on what had transpired and let whatever happened as a result, happen. Steph had overstepped the line, if he paid for it with his life, so be it, Alex would not pay the same price.

"So Alex, why did you inform me of this?" It was the first thing he had said during the entire debrief.

"Sir?"

"It is a simple enough question Alex." He raised a huge eyebrow. "Why did you tell me?"

"Protocol Sir. If Steph wants to fuck up then that's his choice I want no part of it."

"Ah, as I thought." MacLeavey nodded knowingly. "You see Alex, in some people's eyes what you have just done would be seen as treasonous to your friend, Steph is your friend is he not?"

Alex shuffled awkwardly. "Yes Sir."

"However some would also see the virtuosity of Company loyalty. A need for our... employee's," a small grin stole to the edges of his mouth. "to put the Company's interests foremost in whatever they do. This kind of loyalty to the Company should not only be commended but nurtured and encouraged to the utmost." Alex sat proudly with his back straight against the chair, his head back slightly as he basked in the praise. "This loyalty however is absent from you." Before Alex could move metal restraints locked around his arms and legs, on his left arm the metal had painfully pinched a chunk of flesh from him but he knew this was the least of his worries.

"Sir, it wasn't me, I tried to stop Steph..."

MacLeavey raised a finger to his lips and levelled his eyes on Alex. "Stephen's actions today were wrong and he knows this. He still has issues with his sister that he will either resolve or that will cost him his life. He knows this too." MacLeavey rose. "Despite this he appreciates and loves the Company more than anything else he has ever had in his life, with the exception of Jamie of course. Do you think if your positions were reversed, he would be sat there now?"

Alex thought about this. "Yes. Steph would have done the same as me." MacLeavey again smiled.

"You *might*," he leaned closer. "and I emphasise the word *might* very strongly, be correct. If Stephen had come here to report on you it would have been for a different reason to your own. You came here Alex to save your own skin."

"Sir, that's not true, the Company…"

MacLeavey held up his hand to once again silence him. "Yes, yes. The Company requires professionalism and discretion at all times but more than this it requires loyalty." MacLeavey's eyes took on a dangerous glint. "Your decision to come here was little more than an expression of self preservation. Self preservation above loyalty is a very dangerous thing." He drew his face to within an inch of Alex's. "How could we ever trust you not to betray us to an adversary?" Again he raised his eyebrow. MacLeavey clamped his hand over Alex's mouth and nose. Alex tried to struggle but his limbs were held fast and MacLeavey's grip was vice like. "Stephen understands this better than most, perhaps better than any. We allow his indiscretions to an extent because no matter what else he may do he will never betray the Company." With a superhuman effort Alex managed to wrestle his face free. "What if it was to save Jamie!" He managed to gasp before MacLeavey reasserted his grip. "You managed to free your face, the first ever to do so Alex, you should die and feel honoured at that small achievement but then perhaps I am just getting old." Again he leaned close. "You are right of course, about Stephen and his sister Jamie. He would betray us to save her. Fortunately for us you cannot save somebody who is already dead." MacLeavey held his grip for far longer than was required as he stood in thought.

Chapter 39

Annabel stood for a moment looking at the neatly arranged piles before taking one of the huge bath sheets and wrapping it around her. She felt safer wrapped in the towel. Less silly. She took another towel and wrapped it around her hair, walking back in to the lounge. Sebastian was on the phone. He looked up at her as she entered, capturing her with his deep eyes. He held up a finger for her to wait.

"Certainly. No I understand. I will catch the next flight." He pushed the button to hang up the phone. "Feel better?"

Annabel could feel her face redden and not just from the hot water of the shower. "Much." She stated as casually as she could.

Sebastian smiled and gestured to the seat opposite. "Now Annabel, unfortunately I have some urgent business to attend to. Hopefully it will not take more than tonight and maybe tomorrow but it would be better if I were to deal with it in person."

Annabel nodded, feeling the tears come to her eyes, she brushed them away. "I'm sorry."

He knew why she was apologising. "Please, do not be." He moved to sit closer and gently pulled up her chin with his finger so he could look in to her eyes. "The offer to join you in the shower was very… tempting. Very." He looked at he intently. "When I brought you the towels," She looked away unable to look at him. A thought of her writhing in the shower flashed in to her mind. Secretly she wondered if it was in his too. "The temptation was almost overwhelming." She looked back at his smiling face. "We should however be careful. We have only just met. You should not be keen for me to take advantage of your vulnerable situation and I too must be careful to not allow you take advantage of my kindness." He gently patted her stomach in explanation. "Do not mistake my thoughts of you. I do not believe this to be the kind of person you are, however by taking things slowly we shall both be more comfortable about the situation." She nodded in understanding. "Unfortunately I must leave for my flight immediately, I would ask that you dress and Karl will come and collect you personally."

She shuddered slightly at the thought. "Can't I stay here?"

Sebastian smiled. "I want to believe the best of you Annabel, I truly do. However I need to be careful, I would not want to leave you here to abuse my trust, also I would rather know somebody is there to take care of you. Karl will make sure of this." He rose, once again picking up the phone. "If you would not mind getting dressed, Karl shall be here shortly." Annabel nodded, a little consoled, understanding Sebastian's position and drying herself as she walked. Sebastian called after her. "Annabel. When I return we can discuss the shower and perhaps you may be so kind as to extend the invitation again." He smiled mischievously.

Annabel practically skipped down the corridor to the bedroom, already dreaming about the prospect of Sebastian's return. She tried to tell herself not to get carried away but she found she could not help it. Annabel chastised herself, they had only known each other a day, she was being silly. In spite of this her heart refused to calm down, it raced at the possibilities. Someone who genuinely cared for her, for who she was. She would never be hungry again, never cold, never shouted at, demeaned but most importantly *hurt*.

Rotschlossen was waiting for them when they exited the lobby. "Don't you need to pack anything for your trip?" Annabel realised Sebastian had no luggage, he looked a little puzzled and then smiled.

He coughed slightly pretending to clear his throat. "No Annabel that will not be necessary. I shall stay at my place in New York, I have all I need there."

"Oh." Again Annabel was somewhat awed at the vast amount of wealth Sebastian appeared to command. Two days ago she had nowhere to live, Sebastian had at least three places to live and they were just the ones she knew about. They got in to the car.

"Can you take me straight to Heathrow please Karl, I want to be on the next flight."

"Of course Sir."

"Then if you could take Annabel back to the house and make sure she is cared for until my return." Sebastian smiled comfortingly at Annabel.

She could see Karl looking at her in the rear view mirror, once again she felt uncomfortable under his gaze. His words and his smile not seeming to match his eyes. When they arrived at the airport some staff were waiting to meet Sebastian. "Take care Annabel, I shall see you soon. Karl." He nodded to Karl and was immediately ushered away by a group of staff in bright red uniforms. Annabel had never flown before but was reasonably sure it was not normal for someone to be met by so many airport people to board a flight.

--

Sebastian was taken directly to check in, was quickly waved through and took the private elevator to the Upper Class security checkpoint. As he was carrying no luggage he was swiftly through this where he was met by a vehicle which sped him to the gate. As he arrived the last of the economy passengers were boarding. He joined them and was shown to his seat at the front of the plane. He handed his jacket to the stewardess and made himself comfortable for take off.

"Hello Sir. May I get you a drink, maybe some champagne?" Sebastian looked up to see a very attractive brunette stood waiting for his request. As his eyes quickly took in her figure he noted her name badge.

"Hello Chloe. Please call me Sebastian. May I just have a chilled mineral water please?"

"Of course… Sebastian." Her eyes twinkled as she said his name. She returned very shortly with the ice cold water. "There you go Sebastian, if you require *anything* else on the flight this evening, please be sure to let me know." The slight emphasis on the word anything did not go unnoticed and 'Chloe' seemed barely able to contain herself when she rushed back behind the curtains to the galley.

"Oh my God, Karen, have you seen the guy sitting in my section?" Karen looked up from what she was doing. She smiled at the look on Chloe's face. "Someone famous?"

Chloe beamed. "Even better, someone very hot."

Karen discreetly moved past Chloe, whispering as she passed, *"Which seat?"*

"1A"

1A was right next to the curtain, she made a note to scold Chloe for talking so loudly when the gentleman might be able to hear and then caught sight of who was sitting there. "Oh, hello Karen." Sebastian raised his glass of water in her direction as she blushed deeply and waved back. She quickly turned and in hushed tones beckoned Chloe to the other side of the galley.

"Was I right or was I right?"

"Oh you were right, Sebastian is most definitely a fine specimen."

"How do you know his name?"

"He flies this route quite regularly, I've seen him two or three times before, although once was enough to remember him. He is very charming. Exceptionally wealthy too apparently…"

"If he is *that* wealthy though doesn't he have his own private plane?"

"Several… apparently, but sometimes if he has to travel unexpectedly he'll just fly with Virgin."

"Did he say why?"

"I asked him once."

"What did he say?"

"The air hostesses." Giggling they set about preparing the pre-flight procedures.

Chapter 40

Steph had found what he had been looking for. He did not know exact dates but he had approximations based on what Annabel had told him and there was a pattern. He had started with the approximate date Christine had disappeared and then the date Jamie had vanished. When he found the beginnings of a pattern he searched for other possible links. It was difficult, it was like the homeless did not exist. He managed to find two more matches but they were tenuous as the information was so vague, one less so than the other. According to the customs logs around the time of the disappearances Sebastian was out of the country. He had a little more success searching for disappearances around the times when Sebastian was out of the country, but not much more. Nobody cared about the homeless, time did not exist in the same way for them. Rotschlossen's only superior, the only person with the power to keep watch out of the picture. Some of the gaps were starting to be filled in. Now he needed to decide how to proceed. Rotschlossen seemed to inhabit Sebastian's family home just outside the city. *Family home, hmmph family mansion fortress more like.* The thought was sobering. The little information he was able to find out about the house was frightening. The Company were very good at finding information that should not be known. Part of Steph's training involved finding this information. Normally he could put a team on to it for him, perhaps they would have more success, in this situation he did not have the luxury and he doubted how much more intel they would find anyway. He basically knew the layout as it was in 1912 and that there was a lot of security, guards, dogs and autonomous security systems. Private ownership of guns was illegal here of course but he doubted very much he could rely on that.

As he approached his room he knew something was wrong. Running would be pointless if whoever was in the room activated a lockdown he would never make it out of the corridor. He rested his hand on the Sig, still nestled behind his back, pulling it around to his front in a firm double handed grip, he pushed the door open keeping to the side as it soundlessly swung open.

"Enough theatrics Stephen, you can come in." Steph stepped inside and saw MacLeavey with his back to him looking out of the window in to the darkness. "Take a seat Stephen." He turned and casually sat himself down, gesturing to a chair. Steph returned the gun to his belt. MacLeavey had shown no reaction to it's presence and if he wanted Steph dead he would not have made it through the door. "Did you find what you were looking for?"

"Sir?"

"In the computer department. I trust your research was successful?"

"To an extent Sir." There was no point denying it, MacLeavey would know anyway.

"Who do you think killed her?"

Steph was a little taken aback. "You know she's dead?"

"I told you Stephen. We tried looking for her on your behalf. The only reason we would not find her was if she no longer existed." Steph nodded silently. Hearing somebody else confirm his fears made the prospect somewhat more tangible. He had heard it before of course but coming from MacLeavey it was different. MacLeavey would not just assume. MacLeavey was the Company, the Company would not assume. The Company would know.

"Why didn't you tell me sooner?"

"I tried to inform you indirectly Stephen. To tell you outright may have isolated you, destroyed you even."

Steph hesitated, "I think it was Rotschlossen."

MacLeavey raised both eyebrows and drew a slight whistle between his lips. "Karl Rotschlossen... Do you think, or do you know?"

"Believe me Sir, I would much rather it was not him but sometimes even if you don't want to believe in something, you know in your heart it's true." *Jamie.* Her words cut deep, strengthening his resolve.

171

MacLeavey saw the pain in his face. "Jamie's words?"

Steph chuckled, "Yeah, how did you know."

"A bit too sentimental for our sort." Steph nodded in understanding. "I will let you do this Stephen, however there are two conditions."

"Sir." Steph waited. He was not certain he would want to agree to the conditions but he had little choice. The alternative would be him in the ground with a bullet hole in the back of his head and a larger entry wound in the front.

"Firstly, you must not fail. If you are going to kill Karl Rotschlossen then kill him. Do *not* try. Do *not* attempt. He must die, even if it means dying yourself, do you understand?"

"Yes Sir, and the second."

"What second? We never had this conversation Stephen. I am trying to track you down. This is very embarrassing for me and for the Company. One of our operatives has gone rogue and we cannot find him." MacLeavey stood and handed Steph a bag he had not noticed before. Wear this. Get what equipment you need from the supply room but you will need to sort out your own transport. I suggest you use some of your money stash for that." Steph raised a questioning eyebrow. "Please Stephen, as if I would not know. Now you better get going. I will give you an hour before I raise the alarm." Steph did not require a second warning, with a nod of thanks he took the bag and exited the room.

Once MacLeavey was happy Steph had gone far enough he lifted the phone in the room.

"Internal switchboard."

"This is MacLeavey. Notify the Increment that we have reconsidered the Rotschlossen situation and to be prepared for a media blackout."

The phone rang quietly. He placed his cigarette in to the ashtray before lifting the receiver. The Company. Good. He replaced the handset and lifted his cigarette back to his lips. Sebastian and Karl were beginning to think they were untouchable, hopefully this would prove to them otherwise, although for a moment he had thought that maybe they had been right. Nobody had wanted to move against them. Officially nobody was. Officially.

He took a long draw on the cigarette and watched as the flame ignited the Dunhill logo at the base, stopping at the filter. Stubbing it out and exhaling the thick smoke in to an already smoky room he leaned towards the phone to prepare for the media.

Chapter 41

Annabel decided to go straight to sleep once she got to the house. Although she would hardly call it a house. It was gigantic. Security was a lot tighter at the house than the apartment building. Guards manned big electric gates and she saw more guards patrolling the perimeter wall with big dogs. As the car crept virtually without sound except for the gravel crunching under the tires, Karl spoke his first words to her since Sebastian had left for New York. "This is Sebastian's family home, it is from the early 18th century and has several rooms and extensive grounds. It is quite a sight to see, especially during the day." The house was lit with subtle up-lighting, giving a stark appearance to the surrounding darkness. The closest lights were miles in every direction. There were no guards closer to the house. Karl parked the car in a garage to the side of the house and walked around to open the door for Annabel. They left the immaculately clean, white garage and walked across the gravel to the house.

"Are there no guards at the house?"

"None are required. The security between here and the perimeter is substantial, it is exceptionally improbable that anybody could get as far as the house, even if they wanted to." Karl smiled, again it failing to be reflected in his eyes. They entered the house and were stood in a grandiose hall. The big sweeping double staircase would have dominated any other house but in this one it was merely a small part of the entrance. The hall itself was extensive and had several exits leading from it. Karl led her up the staircase, taking the left side, continuing down a corridor, passing through a door, down a second corridor, along to another door. The place was so vast and awe inspiring that Annabel quickly lost any sense of direction, when they finally stopped she realised she had no idea whereabouts in the house she was. "This room has a particularly nice view of the grounds. Tomorrow morning I will meet you for breakfast and show you around the house, it can be a little overwhelming when you first come. We still have some fairly new staff who find themselves heading in the wrong direction."

"Thank you Karl."

"You are welcome Miss Annabel. If you require anything, there is a phone in the room."

"For the staff?"

"No, the staff do not stay most weekends, Sebastian encourages them to visit with their family and friends. No staff are in attendance this weekend, however I shall be available should you require anything. Would there be anything else?"

"No thanks Karl."

"In that case may I bid you a good night Miss Annabel."

"Good night Karl." He turned and walked down the corridor, disappearing almost in an instant. Annabel turned to the luxurious room, closing the door behind her. The plush curtains were flung wide and some of the gardens were visible. The décor looked older and traditional. The kind of fancy décor you would see in those period drama's, Annabel thought. Not what she would expect of Sebastian anyway. *Opulence.* The word came to her suddenly, she couldn't remember quite where she had heard it but that described this room. Too tired to take it all in she stripped down, realising she had no bedclothes she slipped between the sheets of the huge bed naked and fell asleep.

The shadow slipped across the room, the pungent smell already on the cloth. Rotschlossen firmly placed the sodden cloth over Annabel's face. She mumbled a little but never awoke. The house was empty so he could have just dragged her but this way she would remain undamaged. *For now at least.*

Chapter 42

Sebastian felt a hand on his arm gently shaking him awake. He opened his eyes and looked up from his bed to see Chloe leaning over him. The top few buttons of her blouse undone giving a clear view down her top to her breasts. *You have to admire her gumption.* He looked up to her face and sat up.

"Sorry for waking you Sebastian but I have a message for you."

"A message?"

"Yes. A gentleman called Andrew Baxter asks that you call him immediately."

"Thank you Chloe. When and how did you receive this message?"

Chloe looked a little uncertain and looked briefly to the door leading through to the cabin. *"It was sent directly via the captain's radio."*

Sebastian pondered this for only a moment. For Andrew to go to such lengths to contact him it must be important but why had he not contacted Karl? *"Chloe,"* As she leaned close he gently brushed a strand of hair from her face and behind her ear, she visibly blushed, even in the low lighting of the night flight. *"Would you mind getting me some coffee please."*

"O...of course, yes, of course." She stammered and tripped slightly as she stood Sebastian's hand shooting out to steady her. *The things I would do to him...* She thought as she walked back to the galley.

Sebastian pulled the phone from the deposit point under the television terminal. He removed his black American Express card and placed a call directly to Andrew Baxter. The phone was answered halfway through the first ring.

"Baxter."

"Hello Andrew. It appears you have gone to some lengths to contact me."

"Oh God Sebastian, sorry for bothering you, I know you are on a flight and…"

"Andrew. Breathe. You would not have done so unless it was important."

"Of course not, no, why are you whispering?"

"It is a night flight Andrew, most of my travelling companions are asleep."

"Oh right. Anyway, I tried calling Rot… Mr Rotschlossen." He coughed, "But he was not answering the phone or returning my calls."

"What appears to be the problem Andrew."

"Yes, sorry Sebastian. It's just with everything that's been going on over the past 24 hours it was one more thing that seemed very out of place."

Sebastian wondered for a moment what exactly had been going on during the past 24 hours but kept the question to himself. Chloe had returned with his coffee, he took it from her gratefully and returned to the call. *"You are very good at your job Andrew, I expect you above most others to pick up on whether something should be concerning or not."*

"Well… There were some more checks on you and Mr Rotschlossen, around specific dates and times. In particular when you were out of the country on business. Of course it should have raised all manner of flags, especially when the searches about your family home were done."

"You say should have raised flags."

"Well that's why I wanted to speak to you or Mr Rotschlossen, it was as if the computer doing the searches did not exist. I don't mean some schoolboy hacker doesn't exist, I mean literally not there doesn't exist. The computer kicked the data to my email account to look at instead of raising the flags because…"

"We are the only ones that can do it."

177

"Until now at least."

Sebastian thought for a moment. There was one other place that could do it. After all it was Sebastian's company that had supplied the facility to do so, for them to use that facility against them though was unfathomable. Worse, it was virtually an unwritten challenge. *"Has the database been breached?"*

"No. Of course not but I understand your concern. It has no impact on our internal systems just the embedded algorithms in the external servers."

"Andrew can you charter an immediate flight back out of JFK when I land."

"Of course Sebastian."

"Andrew please keep trying Karl."

Chapter 43

Annabel opened her eyes and then immediately closed them again. She had slept very heavily and had woken feeling sick and had a terrible headache. She tried to move her arm to rub her eyes but could not seem to lift it. She tried to sit up but felt pinned down. Taking a deep breath she forced her eyes open again. The headache was less intense this time but the room was completely dark. *I thought I'd left the curtains open.* As her eyes began to adjust she realised there was some light, a dull reflection was coming off of a large screen in front of her. Again she tried to sit up but still could not move her arms. Her stomach suddenly lurched. Her wrists were restrained by some sort of strap. The screen in front of her flashed on showing silent static. The pale light illuminating her terrifying predicament. There were indeed straps on her wrists and her legs were also bound. She was spread eagled on some sort of medical bed.

The static ceased and the face of a young girl came in to focus. The terror was clear in her eyes. *"Please. Let me go. Please."* Her cries echoed around the room. Clearly the darkness hid it's size and the large speakers required to generate that kind of sound. The image cut and the pleas were replaced by sickening screams. The same girl was being shown but the angle was wider. With increasing terror, Annabel realised the girl was strapped to the same bed she was now prisoner upon. A new girl's face replaced the last, the same terror but a certain amount of defiance too. *"You sick fuck. When I get off here I am going to fucking kill you."* Another girl's face appeared, then another, and another. Annabel lost count. Some were abusive, some cried, some tried to shake free, some just screamed. None made any difference. She felt an overwhelming sense of despair. Then she saw her. A face she recognised. *Jamie!* She had decided to go for the breaking down in tears option Annabel thought matter of factly. She felt she may do the same. Another girl she didn't know, it looked like she was throwing a fit, thrashing and trying to escape the straps and then... *CHRISTINE!* Annabel again felt a number of emotions simultaneously. She felt relief at knowing Christine had not abandoned her, guilt for thinking she would do, fear for her friend and what had happened to her and another bout of despair. Christine had decided to shout as much foul mouthed abuse as she could. Annabel actually flinched a little from the tirade, although it helped to strengthen her resolve a little as she proudly watched her friend's aggression but the increase to her resolve was short lived. The screen changed again. She recognised the girl on there now too. It was her. She was being shown this so she knew, no matter how she acted, the result would be the same. Annabel was going nowhere.

Chapter 44

Shortly after the plane touched down Chloe escorted him through the airport to the section for privately chartered flights. Sebastian's plane would be waiting. She had been very accommodating. "Do you really have to leave immediately?"

He smiled in the disarming way he did and Chloe blushed. "Unfortunately so Chloe, I have imp…" Two US Customs officials were approaching and quickly cut him off.

"I'm sorry people but you must clear this area immediately."

Sebastian knew from experience that arguing with customs officials in any country was cause for unnecessary trouble. The US border police even more so. Normally he did not allow this to bother him as he understood better than most what a difficult job they had to do under even more difficult conditions however it was vital he was able to return to the UK immediately. The US officials were already herding them back down the corridor. "Is there a problem gentlemen?"

One of them gave a wry smile "Unfortunately Sir but it is nothing for you personally to worry about. Ma'am are you in attendance to a specific flight?"

"I was escorting this gentleman to a privately chartered connecting flight. It is essential that he gets to the plane as quickly as possible."

The officials looked at each other. "Did no one tell you? There has been a terrorist alert the entire airport is being locked down."

Sebastian remained calm as he immediately knew the futility of arguing. He considered for a moment contacting a suitably high up friend but since September 11th this kind of action was taken incredibly seriously and was unlikely to have any substantial impact. "Is it just JFK that is in lockdown?" The officers had started herding them back down the corridor again.

"No Sir."

"Sebastian, please."

"No Sebastian, it's all airports in the tri-state area. Nobodies goin' nowhere. Please through here." The officers showed them through a door in to a security clearance area. "Take care."

"My apologies may I just ask one more thing."

"Shoot."

"Is there any indication of how long the lockdown is likely to last?"

The officer looked grim. "Could be anything from a couple to several hours, we have no indication yet."

"Thank you for your help."

"Hey, no problem." They closed and locked the door leaving Sebastian and Chloe stood on the other side. *The wrong side.* He took a deep breath and closed his eyes. Chloe looked at him worriedly.

"Hey Chloe." It was Karen, she walked over with Chloe's case a look of worry on her face. "I take it you didn't make it Sebastian. The airport alert went off almost immediately after you left the plane."

"Does anyone know what's going on?"

"No. After you and Sebastian left the plane we received orders that everyone was to clear the plane as quickly as possible. You can imagine the chaos that caused. Customs is virtually in chaos there are so many people waiting. Even the VIP and flight crew lines are full."

"I may be able to do something about that, excuse me." Sebastian decided to make the call after all. Chloe watched him walking away.

"Close your mouth Chloe."

She poked her tongue out at Karen playfully. "Oh Karen I want to have his babies."

"You decided this after 6 hours on the plane?" Chloe looked meaningfully at her. "Okay you win. I want to have his babies too." They laughed together again.

"What do you think he meant about being able to do something about the queues?"

"Beats me."

As if on cue Sebastian returned with an officer from the US Border Patrol. "Ladies, this is Brad. He is kindly going to escort us through security."

Karen and Chloe stood open mouthed. "During an airport lockdown?"

"Yes Chloe, during an airport lockdown."

"If you'd all kindly follow me." Brad had a thick Italian American accent, a true New Yorker. They followed him through a door marked authorised personnel only.

Ten minutes later they were stood outside the airport. "Thank you both for your help, I need to get to my New York apartment. I will have to travel straight there but if you would like my driver to take you anywhere afterwards then you are more than welcome to accompany me." The limousine pulled up and the girls could barely contain themselves. The driver came around to open the door and Sebastian patiently waited until they climbed in. The driver closed the door and quickly loaded the cases in to the already open boot. Before speeding off in to the New York traffic.

Chloe looked wantonly at Sebastian. "Does this mean you are staying a little bit longer than you thought?" She was practically purring and Karen cringed ever so slightly, shaking her head and hiding her smile behind her hand.

"As much as I wish it were otherwise Chloe, I am afraid I do not have time for what you and Karen are thinking. At least I am hoping I do not in the nicest possible way. I can do a certain amount from my New York office however as soon as the airport lockdown is lifted I must return to the UK immediately." Chloe looked somewhat disappointed, Karen breathed a sigh of relief and stopped furiously twisting her wedding ring.

The car came to a halt in front of a towering skyscraper in what seemed moments later. Sebastian looked back in to the car and smiled. "Until next time ladies, the driver shall take you wherever you wish." He closed the door and the car eased off in to the traffic at a more reserved pace. As Sebastian turned to the entrance Dick Adamski was standing ready to take him inside. Adamski had worked for the New York office for the last 11 years, Sebastian remembered him being appointed as Director of Operations for the New York office about 6 years ago, it was one of the last major appointments his father had made before he died.

"Sebastian, thank god you're here. I've had Andrew Baxter on the phone since late last night. What the hell is going on?"

"Calm yourself Dick. There was a minor security breach in the United Kingdom, however the specific breach in question is of sufficient importance to imply quite a serious problem with one of our clients."

Adamski did not ask any further questions, Baxter withholding the information from him was sufficient cause for alarm and if Sebastian was not going to clarify any further he reasoned it wasn't his place to ask. "Your office is ready, we have a video conference link with London on a secure encrypted signal so you can talk with Baxter."

"Thank you Dick, however talking with Andrew is of little use to me if it is what I think it is. I will need to speak directly to one of our clients in the United Kingdom, in person. Could you please monitor the airport lockdown, use whatever resources you require and have a helicopter ready to go on the roof as soon as the no fly zone restriction is lifted over the city."

"Yes Sebastian, I will take care of it personally."

"Dick. *Whatever* resources you require. I cannot stress the importance of getting back to the United Kingdom immediately."

Adamski nodded his understanding and again heard the voice inside him panic slightly at the situation he did not entirely understand. "I know this is probably not a priority at the moment Sebastian but what shall I do about the Beaumont meeting, he was expecting to see you in person."

"If I find I am still here I shall meet with them briefly to apologise in person, however this current situation is to take utmost priority over everything else."

"Understood." Adamski sped away to take care of Sebastian's requests upon reaching the door to Sebastian's office.

He opened the door and entered the perfectly climate controlled room. Upon closing the door he knew that it was completely sealed and that no noise would enter, or more importantly, escape. He stood in front of the flat screen monitor that covered most of one of the walls. "Andrew."

Immediately Baxter's haggard face appeared on the screen. "Sebastian thank god."

"Hello Andrew. Have you been able to make any progress?"

"No. Unfortunately not. I have tried pretty much everything I could think of and everything I couldn't too."

"Okay Andrew. I need you to try something for me. May I ask have you confirmed that this connection is completely secure or shall I check?"

"I've been running constant checks while I have waited for you but in light of what has happened I can't be sure."

"Do not start doubting yourself Andrew. You are very skilled at what you do. Listen very carefully to my instructions, I will require you to implement the code directly from the primary computer."

Andrew listened as Sebastian started relaying the complicated instructions. Much of it he understood but some parts were completely new to him and as he began to grasp some realisation of what he was constructing his mouth dropped in awe of Sebastian. Once completed, Sebastian patiently repeated everything again so Andrew was able to check it. The code was beautiful. He could understand why Sebastian was so keen for a secure connection and had not just forwarded the code to him by email, he could also see why Sebastian had rather been present to input the code himself. Andrew considered himself a very adept programmer, it was one of the reasons Sebastian and Rotty held him in such esteem, *but this!* Again, he marvelled at the code with wonder.

Sebastian finished repeating everything back to Baxter. "Is all as it should be Andrew?"

"Yes Sebastian." Baxter breathed with reverence. "I'm sure this is accurate to the character as you've relayed it to me."

"Andrew I wish for you to compile and run the code. Be careful not to let it fall in to anybody else's hands." Baxter nodded his assurance. "It will take some time to run to completion. I shall wait here until you return unless the flight restrictions are lifted."

"Of course Sebastian." Baxter disappeared from the screen. Sebastian sat back in his chair, clasping his hands together. He lifted his index fingers in to a point and rested the tips against his lips as he sat deep in thought. His face did not betray any anger, worry or concern. His face remained impassive, only Sebastian knew his thoughts.

Chapter 45

"WHAT DO YOU WANT FROM ME?!?" Her scream resonated around the room and Annabel burst in to tears. The screen turned black and somewhere she heard contented laughter. The voice was one she recognised. It was as she had suspected. Karl Rotschlossen. The confirmation caused her skin to break out afresh in goose bumps. *Sebastian.* Her mind desperately held to thoughts of him. He was her last chance she knew. The only person who could possibly stop this madman. She prayed he would return soon from his trip.

Annabel had lost all sense of time, she did not know if it was minutes, hours or days before the screen flashed on again. Once again with the image of a young girl. She vaguely recognised her as the one that had appeared first last time. Still strapped to the bed as Annabel was now. Then the horrific abuses began. The girl on the screen looked up with wide eyed disbelief and terror as a shadow fell over her. The shape of a man moved on to the screen, his face obscured but Annabel knew it must be Rotschlossen. She closed her eyes as she saw the man approach the terrified girl but no matter how tightly she closed her eyes it could not block out the screams. Annabel desperately wished she could free her hands so she could clamp them over her ears, like she had when she was young. When Rory used to shout at her. The shackles held fast though. Through teary eyes she watched the screen again, she had not noticed it change to another girl. She was gagging as the man forced himself in to her throat, releasing over her face and in to her eyes. The girl writhed and blinked furiously as she sobbed and tried to clear her vision. She gasped in surprise and relief as the man released one of her shackles but he immediately pulled her arm over to her other side, twisting her body painfully and shackling her arm next to the one on the other side. He forced her up on to her knees. The scream she released as he forced himself between her buttocks brought Annabel's eyes closed instinctively. This time she heard every sob and cry, she knew when the footage of this girl had changed to the next.

The screams began afresh.

Time no longer held any meaning for her as the screams continued, different girls causing them each time. Some begged to be released, others just cried or screamed. Those who offered themselves willingly were more violently abused than those that struggled, until they too began to strain and struggle. The more they struggled the more it seemed to please the brute abusing them. Annabel seethed with wrath at Rotschlossen. She vomited until her stomach was empty. The acidic smell stinging her eyes as it clung to her and the bombardment of the images on the screen continued relentlessly. After she had vomited her stomach dry, she cried tears until she could cry no more. She stopped straining, her eyes hurt from the tears and from forcing them so tightly closed. The noise and images washed over her now, almost without impact. Only the most brutal abuses causing her to flinch. Her eyes drifted closed, opening occasionally when a particularly severe and bloodcurdling scream was released by any of the girls. Annabel felt guilt at trying to ignore what had been done to them but was desperately clawing at the hope Sebastian would return in time to save her. *Had he known about these girls? Surely if he had he'd have been suspicious of Rotschlossen? Please Sebastian, please come home. Save me.* She could feel the last vestiges of her sanity clawing at some semblance of reality. Annabel was finding it increasingly difficult to keep herself from the pit of despair that was dangerously close to overwhelming her completely. She had seen some of the girls had completely lost their sanity during the attacks. *Rapes.* She corrected herself bitterly. As the tears began to flow once more the screams subsided once again as the next girls torment began. Annabel froze as the words, even at the high volume she knew the sound was being blasted in to the room, barely audible, whispered their way to her ears. Annabel forced open her eyes to look upon the face as she whispered the words again and again, a mantra that would somehow protect her. *"Even if you do not want to believe something, in your heart you know it's true. Even if you do not want to believe something, in your heart you know it's true. Even if you do not want to believe something, in your heart you know it's true."* Jamie had clearly lost her sanity. Her eyes were vacant and the man was brutally attacking her but the words kept being whispered, over and over. He grabbed at her breasts, squeezing them so forcefully she knew it must be excruciating, pulling her hair so hard the skin was pulled taught in her face. No respect was given for the sensitive areas he penetrated, Annabel could see blood seeping from those areas and through her catharsis, Annabel's heart ached with the need to help her and the agony of knowing it had already been done and there was nothing she could do to help her. She forced herself not to watch it all but sounds still sickened her.

Apparently tiring of her the man stopped and the image of her face filled the screen. Her lips barely moving, soundless now but still mouthing the mantra. *"Even if you do not want to believe something, in your heart you know it's true."*

The grief that overwhelmed her meant she hardly noticed the torture of the next girl until the image faded, it was then that Annabel felt fresh pain as she realised who would be next.

Christine!

Chapter 46

Sebastian remained impassive as Baxter returned to the screen. He immediately noticed the flustered look on his face.

"Hello Andrew. I trust that the program has run its course?"

"Sebastian... I..."

"Andrew, you know that I like you and have a great deal of trust and respect in your abilities however you must learn to control your nerves. It is not constructive to be so unable to control your emotions."

"Please accept my apologies Sebastian but the results..."

"The results Andrew are the results. They are no more and they are no less."

"The program successfully back traced to a point but was unable to resolve the original host. Nothing I know of exists that would be able to hide from the program you recited to me."

"Andrew, please do not accept this as an attack of your abilities however an hour ago you were unaware something such as the program could exist."

Baxter seemed to consider this before continuing. "But Sebastian, when the program completed I was afraid I had made a mistake so I recompiled it to trace something else..."

"What did you choose to test it upon?"

"The Department of Defence scan from last month. It took less than 30 seconds and gave full data. I chose the DoD because the trace went via Akamai Technologies, unlike the DoD trace though it pretty much stopped. The program estimated a location for the source to a location just outside London, about 20 miles from here, to the north west."

"51 degree's, 35 minutes and 26 seconds North by 0 degree's 26 minutes and 48 seconds West, a white farmhouse with a long tarmac drive backing on to some woods?"

Baxter was taken aback once more. "Yes, how could you..? But if you knew then why go to all this trouble?"

"Andrew my dear friend, there is a difference between suspecting something and knowing something. I merely suspected before, now I know."

"Sebastian there is very little information about this place but it appears to be just some waste management company."

"Indeed it does." Sebastian was silent for a moment. "Andrew I will be on the next possible flight out of New York. Would you please continue to try and contact Karl?"

"Of course Sebastian."

There was a knock at the door and a tired looking Adamski entered. "Sebastian, sorry for interrupting but you said if you were still here you would meet with William Beaumont."

"Thank you Andrew, that will be all for now." He turned his attention back to Adamski. "Am I to understand that the flight restriction is still in force?"

"Yes Sebastian."

Sebastian nodded. "Then it would be unnecessary for me to not meet with Bill. I trust he is in the executive meeting room?" Adamski gave a curt nod. "Let us not keep Bill waiting any longer then." Sebastian walked briskly down the corridor. The shouting could be heard from some distance away.

"You tell Sebastian that it's disgusting he should keep me waiting like this. Don't you dare try to hush me my boy or I'll fillet you like a fish. Don't you know who I am, can somebody please get someone who knows what the hell things are about." Sebastian walked around the corner. A slight smile stole to his lips momentarily. "SEBASTIAN! Where in the devil have you been. We have a problem with our software!"

"Good evening Bill."

The colour drained from William Beaumont's face. "Evening? EVENING!? It's the early hours of the morning!"

"Yes, I suppose it is. Unfortunately I was unable to get here any sooner Bill, I was only notified of the urgency to see you late last night Greenwich Mean Time." Before he could start off in another tirade Sebastian placed his hand on Bill's shoulder and guided him towards the plush furnishings of the meeting room. "Shall we discuss this in private Bill?" Grunting in agreement Beaumont glowered at the staff that had been trying to pacify him prior to Sebastian's arrival. He sat down heavily in a plush chair as Sebastian closed the door.

He shouted loudly at Sebastian. "Is this room sound proof from those prying ears outside. I don't want every rat in 30 miles to know the vulnerabilities I'm exposed too!"

"Even to your loudest shouts Bill."

"You're sure?"

"Yes Bill, I am sure. If you were to stop shouting you could be surer still."

His face took on a fatigued and heavy look. A weight of responsibility came over his face. He took a deep breath and leaned forward conspiratorially. "Sorry for the outburst Sebastian but I had to make a good show of things. I have some vital information to give you. Forces are moving against you."

Chapter 47

Steph arrived at the grounds, it was a little after 8am. It had taken longer than he thought to get what he needed but Rotschlossen was here and Steph was going to make sure that today would be his last. The security was exceptionally tight around the grounds so he had decided he would only enter if he really needed to. *Better to let him come to me.* He had ditched his car some distance away and hiked in on foot. Although the ground appeared to start at the perimeter wall he had known they started much further away than that. The security sensors had started a good two miles away from where the grounds appeared to start and an abandoned car would have given him away. On the plus side the grounds only had one road for access and therefore, for exit. Unless Rotschlossen decided to fly out by helicopter he would have to go down this road. Steph would be waiting.

The morning turned in to late morning and then in to early afternoon. Steph remained concealed where he was, eating some rations. *What the hell is he doing in there?* He puzzled over why Rotschlossen had not left the building, it seemed unlikely he would not be needed at work considering the position he held. The only vehicles that passed were the minibuses transporting the guards to and from their shifts. He began to panic that Rotschlossen had maybe used one of these to leave the house but reasoned this was extremely unlikely and to focus on the job at hand.

Every muscle in Steph's body tensed as a minibus with fresh guards slowed as it approached his position, it stopped less than 200 feet away. A guard got off the bus, appeared to kick the front tire, cursed then climbed back inside. The other guards all climbed off the bus and the guard that had originally got off appeared with a jack and a tyre iron. As some gave him a hand to change the tyre other's wandered off a little way to smoke.

"Too bloody cold to be out here."

"You're not wrong G much rather be up at the mansion bet it's nice and snug in there."

"I don't know about that, Rotty's in there."

He paused in thought for a second. "You're right, on second thoughts I think I'll brave the cold." The two guards laughed, Steph continued to maintain the grip on his trusty Sig. If they discovered him now he was screwed, even with the silencer. A shout came from the minibus and the two guards returned to it. It drove off past Steph without further incident. *Well at least I know Rotschlossen is still at the house!* He thought.

Steph continued to wait. He could only wait for so long. MacLeavey had told him that the Company would be after him, he was surprised they had not found him yet. It's not like they did not know where he was going. A niggle of doubt entered his mind briefly but he quickly dismissed it. Steph started to mentally go over the plan he had hoped he would not have to use. If Rotschlossen did not make an appearance by twilight he would have to go in and get him.

Chapter 48

Annabel felt emotionally destroyed.

She had wanted more than anything to close her eyes and ears to the torment Christine had been going through on the screen in front of her. Nothing had been sacred, no part of her body, no sexual act. Annabel had realised that she did not know if all the girls had been treated the same way as this was the only one she had watched fully, although she had seen most of what happened to Jamie. Flashes of the things that had been inserted in to Christine came to her mind and she felt her skin crawl. She instinctively tried to pull her legs together to shield herself but the restraints made it impossible.

Once again she lay in the darkness waiting for the inevitable to happen to her. The smell of stale vomit and urine overwhelming her senses. The sudden silence both a relief and oppressively foreboding.

Chapter 49

Sebastian sat across from William Beaumont. "You are sure of this Bill?"

He sighed and nodded slowly. "Sebastian our families have been friends for generations. Your father was one of the best, no he was the best, friend I have had the honour to know. I am sure."

Sebastian had sat silently while Beaumont had told him what he knew. Finding some information too sensitive to communicate except in person and knowing that a sudden trip by himself to London would have been suspicious he had used a minor problem with some software as an excuse to bring Sebastian to him. A friend of his in the Pentagon had warned Beaumont to distance himself from Sebastian as elements of the British government were growing concerned of his ever increasing international power and influence. Some believed that a lesson was required to remind Sebastian that he was not invincible, not God. The flight restriction over New York was implemented by an anti-terror task force within the British government, conveniently late enough so Sebastian's flight would not be diverted to another airport but early enough that he would be unable to leave again.

Sebastian's jaw had tightened at this, he did not like being trapped. "I thank you for the risk you have taken in bringing this to my attention Bill however I think we may be too late. Those that move against me would only seek to trap me here if it was to their benefit. If they wish to make a move against me they shall do so while I am unable to stand against them, while I am trapped here." Beaumont nodded, a pained expression upon his face. "Perhaps between us we may be able to improve the present situation somewhat. If the flight restriction was put in to place by intelligence received from the British government then it shall not be released by them until after they have achieved what they wish."

"Agreed."

"The very restrictions they seek to restrict me with also helps to make clear my choices as they are so limited. Either I shall wait for the restriction to be lifted and sort through whatever chaos they have wreaked in my absence upon my return, leave New York and endeavour to fly from somewhere else, or I use this power and influence they fear so much to return against their wishes. I must say I favour the final option above all others." He had a dangerous glint in his eye and smirk on his lips.

"You are indeed your Father's son Sebastian."

"Bill I would greatly appreciate it if you could also lend me some of your influence in this matter. I intend to leave for Britain today and would rather do it with the support of the United States Air Force and not their persecution. "Bill's face regained some of his colour and he smiled. "Shall we start with your friend at the Pentagon?"

Chapter 50

Rotschlossen once again turned off the screen. Watching the images again had aroused him greatly but he refused to act on those urges. He stubbornly suppressed them, instead reminding himself of how much better it would be if he waited until Annabel was ready.

The meddlesome little bitch!

The thought carried so much venom he could almost feel the spittle fly from the mental image of his mouth. He smirked at this. The girl was a disgusting mess, he could see before he had turned the screen off that the dirty little whore had relieved herself all over the bed. Her hair was all matted with the contents of her stomach. He would have to take care of that of course. Working a touch-screen control station he released gas in to the chamber. It was designed to release slowly so Annabel would have the sensation of falling asleep. He enjoyed playing mind games with the girls, preparing them. He enjoyed the panic in them when they would wake and realised things had changed that should have awoken them from their sleep.

He decided she could lay there suffering in her filth for the moment. He loathed these girls. They were gutter scum. Troublesome. Dirty and this one in particular, problematic. He used to think that maybe it was not their faults they had ended up in this situation but he had been trying to fool himself he knew. It was their fault. They had chosen to live like so much trash. They had chosen to make themselves so vulnerable and miss able. They might as well have spread their own legs and strapped themselves to the bed. He watched the monitors as Annabel's racing heart beat slowed and her breathing returned to a more normal, regular pace. He waited a little longer to make sure she was asleep before clearing the gas. The compound was extremely effective and would render her unconscious for several hours.

He entered the chamber and did what was required before returning to the control room. It had been a long night so he decided to climb in to the bed he kept there and catch some sleep. The girl would wait he reasoned, she was not going anywhere.

Karl awoke and stretched, some of his muscles clicking as he did so. He stood and flicked a switch to turn on some soft lights in the chamber. He entered unhurriedly and walked to a bath tub at the back of the room that had previously been hidden in the darkness. Karl turned on the taps and added some fragrant bath salts. He sat on the side of the bath and absently stirred the water with his fingers. Happy with the temperature he turned his attention to the unconscious form of Annabel still strapped down.

He methodically undid the straps and tenderly lifted her from the bed, carrying her over to the bath. Karl gently lowered her in to the water, the acidic smell of the vomit and urine mingling with the soft lavender from the bath salts. He gently began massaging shampoo in to her hair, washing the harsh smells away. He followed this with a conditioner and rich smelling oils. Slowly. Methodically. Carefully he clipped and shaved her pubic hair, doing the same with her legs.

Karl pulled a padded towel from a cupboard and lay it on the floor before lifting Annabel's now clean and glistening form from the bath. Water ran in rivulets over her naked body, dripping in to the tub below. He held her easily, she weighed next to nothing to him. As the dripping and the echoes of it slowly dissipated he turned and lowered her on to the padded towel. Turning once again he collected another clean towel. Gently he stroked it across her body, careful to thoroughly dry her but without rubbing hard enough to redden the skin.

Once satisfied Annabel was dry enough Karl once again returned to the cupboard, this time removing a tub. He unscrewed the lid and the sweet smell of vanilla body butter drifted to his nose. He knelt beside her and gently massaged the cream in to her body. Once again, taking his time, making certain that it was all absorbed, that no oily sheen remained, that skin was smooth, nourished and healthy. Satisfied with his work, he removed the clothing that had already been selected and with the same great care, he dressed her.

He stood over her peaceful form for a moment, looking down at her. Slowly he once again stopped and lifted her in to his arms. Crossing the room in long purposeful strides and gently laying her back on the bed, strapping her back in to her restraints.

He waited for her to awake.

Chapter 51

Steph had been watching the house all day and there had been no change. He felt irritable as he began to realise that he was going to have no choice but to access the house directly. He had nowhere near as much intelligence as he would have liked to attempt this kind of assault, especially on somewhere like this. At least the time spent waiting had given him time to watch the guard rotations. He estimated that if he waited for the change of guard he would have four hours before the next change. Normally a change would be a moment of weakness but here it seemed to be the moment of most danger. They had been well drilled and were careful to make sure that there was never even a momentary lapse in security. The guards watch was carefully overlapped to allow time for the new guards to become accustomed to their post and the previous guards to convey any incident, no matter how trivial, to them. They were extremely well disciplined. They did not engage in idle chatter, not because they were afraid too but because they were trained to concentrate entirely on the task at hand. They were also heavily armed but that was not his biggest concern. The dog patrols were extensive and like the guards, exceptionally well trained. He knew that to underestimate the security was likely to cost him his life. *I had better make sure I do not underestimate the security then.*

Chapter 52

Annabel awoke. Her mind was slightly foggy and she was surprised that she had been able to sleep after experiencing such a nightmare of an ordeal. With her eyes still closed she thought that perhaps it had all been a dream after all. The restriction as she tried to move her arms confirmed that it was not a dream, she was still a captive. As her mind began to clear she realised there was an itching sensation in her hand and a sweet perfume smell from somewhere. She was shocked to realise the sweet smell was herself. The vomit and urine had been cleaned from her. She recoiled at the thought of Rotschlossen touching her when she had no way to stop him or at the very least show her revulsion to it. To her side she could see the slight silhouette of a metal pole. She could not see where the small amount of light was coming from but it was enough to make out the rest of the shape, it was a drip. Again Annabel felt fear, this was the itching on the back of her hand, what could he have put in to her. Poison? That seemed a bit pointless. Then what? Her mind was confused, she was tired still. Although she had slept it was an unnatural forced sleep and her mind ached from continually being drugged. As her mind cleared completely she began to wish that the effect had lingered as the memories of the screen returned. Her mind brought forth an image of Christine unbidden. Her screams, her soft flesh tearing. She whimpered slightly at the knowledge it was going to happen to her. She had seen their resolve broken and then she had seen them used and discarded as if they were nothing. There was nothing left to see, he would be coming for her soon she knew. She braced herself in an attempt to steel her resolve against what was to come, she promised to fight back with everything she had. If he came anywhere near her face with that thing she would tear at it with her teeth until they were all smashed from her skull. Her anger was short lived though, quickly being replaced by fear. She had seen the same resolve in the eyes of the others quickly melt away to be replaced by fear, the fear that to do anything to upset the beast attacking them would only draw out and somehow make the attack worse.

The dark screen again flared to life. Annabel's eyes slowly focused on the image. It was the girl she had come to recognise as appearing first. A trickle of cold sweat ran down her neck and between her shoulder blades where it soaked in to some cloth. She looked down and realised she had also been dressed. She vaguely realised that some of the girls in the video had either changed their clothes during the ordeal or gone from being naked to clothed, only to have the garments torn from them. Her attention returned to the screen as with morbid apprehension she waited to see what was still left for this poor girl to be subjected too. She watched as she was slapped around the face, apparently in an attempt to bring her out of the daze she was in. Then the screams started once more. The poor girl, who had already suffered so much, who had already been broken emotionally beyond anything anybody could or should be expected to endure was to be completely broken physically too. Although Annabel felt the rising bile in the back of her throat there was still nothing for her to vomit as she watched the torture. Skin, eyelashes, eyes, lips, tongue, nipples…each was destroyed by the monster on the screen. At the end, the girl still writhing in agony, her screams barely more than a hoarse whisper, a knife was slowly pushed between her breasts, the audible crack of the breastplate echoing within the chamber both from the speakers and in the present. Blood spattered from her mouth as the blade was inserted and levered backwards and forwards, her head becoming limp and hanging to the side as the heart was removed. With a small scalpel a word was etched in to the fleshy side of the heart. *Whore.* The screen lingered with the lifeless face of the girl, her eyes permanently open from where the lids had been removed, staring without purpose at Annabel. The screen darkened momentarily and the next girl appeared.

Chapter 53

Steph had finally made it in to the house, he was sweating and itching slightly from the suit MacLeavey had given him. It seemed to be made of some sort of hardened polymer and was skin tight. He had promised himself he would not underestimate the security he would encounter. As soon as he had breached the outside perimeter he realised how close he had come to failing. In his time with the company he had been tasked with entering some extremely secure and sensitive areas undetected. He could unquestionably state this was the most secure he had seen and that included the company premises. Getting to the house had been one of the most difficult challenges he had faced. Getting in to the house *was* the most difficult.

It was clear the house was completely locked down. All entrances were impassable. The "glass" in the windows was made of reinforced triple layered Perspex the best Steph could tell. The only one he was able to enter through gave him the feeling that it was a deliberate ease of access point for emergencies. *Ease of access. Humph.* Steph smiled slightly at his thoughts. It had been far from easy, he just hoped that now he was in the house the security would be slightly less, on the basis that those inside were meant to be there. He still had no idea where to look for Rotschlossen. Steph was assuming he would be asleep, no lights were visible from outside but the whole house was a maze. From above it would look like a large square with a garden in the middle. There were several rooms in each wing of the three storey building and Steph knew from the old plans that there had been some underground chambers as well, although it seemed likely they were used for storage, if Rotschlossen had a study for example under the house, he may be there. Steph stopped for a moment and rubbed his temples with his index fingers, he had to think. There was not enough time to stealthily search the entire building but it seemed to be the only way to be sure. The other option was to create a large enough incident to catch Rotschlossen's attention and draw him out but this was likely to bring the entire security force down on him at the same time.

As he stood with his eyes closed and his fingers pressed against his temples he noticed something he had not before. It was like a hum, or maybe a vibration, he was not sure exactly what it was but he could feel it. It reminded him of the feeling when a neighbour plays really loud music but without the noise. It was so subtle that, if it was not for the completely deserted house and being stood in the dark with his eyes closed, he would not have noticed. Steph stood trying to get a feel of where it was coming from, it seemed to be everywhere at once but as he was able to tune out everything else he realised it was coming from below. *Down it is then.* He began his search for the basement.

Chapter 54

Karl sat comfortably in the chair watching Annabel as she watched , or tried to avoid watching the screen. The girl knew her fate, at least she thought she did. Seeing and living something were quite different, as she would soon find out.

As his mind wandered he realised he had not received any calls since last night. It was unusual as Sebastian would normally have phoned to confirm he had landed okay. He reached for the phone and realised it was not where he would normally have placed it. Karl mentally retraced his steps and he concluded he must have left it in his room. He checked his watch, it was about 20 hours since he had left his room, he was sure nothing much could have happened in this time but he felt he should really go and collect it just in case. This posed a dilemma for him, should he stop the footage? No it would spoil the impact. The girl was restrained, she would be unable to know he had left, he would have time to return before it had ended.

Karl stood and went through the door in the rear of the control room, the screams following him as he walked down the corridor.

Chapter 55

Steph jumped at the sudden noise. He had been trying to follow the strange sensation but largely to no avail. The basement appeared to only be for storage. Bottles of wine, smoked meats, barrels of whiskey. He was exploring a corner when he heard the spine-chilling scream. Although muffled, in the silence it was both unexpected and loud. The screams continued and he searched his way through the catacombs of the basement. He found a door he had not seen previously, hidden behind one of the wine racks but now ajar. Removing his Sig he gently nudged the door open to see a spiral staircase leading down. The screams were louder now and were coming from below. He slowly edged his way down the stairs.

Chapter 56

Annabel had largely avoided watching the images on the screen but she could do nothing to block out the sounds. Once again she cried until her eyes stung and she could cry no more. Her cheeks felt cold with the moisture that had soaked them. The last lot of images that had been paraded in front of her were awful and sickening, this was the same but more so and in an even more sadistic and evil way. *Evil. Yes,* she decided. *That's exactly what this is.* Although she had shunned the visual bombardment the screen forced upon her to a large degree, she had seen enough to know that it always ended the same way. The girl's heart would be cut out while she was still alive and then words carved in to the heart to describe the girl. Whore. Slut. Bitch. Filth. Street scum. The degradation finally coming to an end for each of them in life but being continued with the recordings in death. Her eyes sealed shut she realised that she was once again approaching the end.

"Even if you do not want to believe something, in your heart you know it's true."

The hoarse whisper rang clearly through the room. The screams were short to follow.

Chapter 57

Steph caught his breath. He had neared the bottom of the staircase and was moving cautiously forwards when he heard the words; *"Even if you do not want to believe something, in your heart you know it's true."* One thought filled his mind. *Jamie.* She must still be alive. The screams that followed the words caused him to throw any sense of caution to the wind. He jumped the last few steps and crashed through the door in to the control room waving his gun wildly.

The sight on the screen in front of him stopped him in his tracks.

Jamie!

He watched as the blade cut in to his little sisters flesh and heard her screams as the life was lacerated from her body. The man holding the knife had deftly removed a large section of her skin from her shoulder, chest and her right breast, he was now toying with the exposed nerve endings sending shudders of pain through the body. *No not a body. Jamie's!* Steph dropped to his knees in front of the screen, he had seen and done many terrible things in his work for the Company but he had never made or seen anyone suffer like this. He was unable to tear his eyes away as he watched his sister's mutilation. Only an unhinged monster could do this to another human being. *Especially a defenceless little girl like Jamie.*

Steph vomited heavily on to the floor. He pushed himself up and leaned against the wall, then vomited again. He felt the acid burning the back of his throat and also felt a second burning. His anger, his hatred, Rotschlossen was going to pay for this. His head swam but his anger helped him to block out the screams and focus. He looked through the thickly paned windows in front of him in to a chamber where a large screen had been mounted. Beneath it he could see a young woman strapped to a bed. *Like Jamie.* Was it Jamie? No it couldn't be. He looked closer and felt a chill as he recognised the girl lying on the bed.

Chapter 58

Annabel felt numb again. She had thought that her abuse was about to start only to find that what was to come first was only the beginning. How she was to die made her truly petrified. She could hear the gurgling of Jamie choking on her own blood and knew that her heart was being removed. She opened her eyes and flinched as she saw a dark figure approaching her. The resolve she had forged to fight with everything she had immediately dissolved as she knew it would. The screen, still occupying most of her vision displayed Jamie's heart. The words for her carved deep in to it. As the figure reached the side of the bed, the maniacal laughter from the speakers caused him to turn his head to see the joke. Annabel wept with relief at the sight of Steph's blacked up face but also with despair at the sick joke of the words carved in to the heart. In deep, bold capital letters were the words; *IT'S TRUE.*

Chapter 59

Karl unhurriedly proceeded to his room, he found his mobile where he had left it beside the bed. He was getting old. In all his years of service he could never remember forgetting his phone since they had been available. He picked it up and looked at it. He was confused to see that the battery was dead, he had not charged it since yesterday but he had made no calls so found it strange that the battery should be depleted.

He reached behind the bedside cabinet and pulled out the thin wire to charge the phone. Once the charging indicator appeared he turned it on and placed it on the bed, strolling over to the window to look out over the grounds. It got so dark, so early in the winter. The phone finished loading up, then, finding a signal started vibrating furiously. He went over to examine the phone and was shocked to discover numerous missed calls. He also had several text messages and voicemails. The missed calls were from Baxter, Sebastian's mobile, the London office, the New York office. Karl immediately dialled Sebastian's number, he waited as it connected but it was diverted to voicemail. Next he tried Baxter. It was answered on the first ring. "Baxter I have…"

"Rotschlossen where the hell have you been, we've been trying to get hold of you for the past 24 hours."

Karl was somewhat taken aback, Baxter had never dared to speak to him like this before, something was wrong. "I am at the house, why did you not send someone over if it was that important?"

"We tried, but there was no response from the house and it was entirely locked up. The guards were certain you were inside but nobody had seen or heard from you. With the house locked up the guards had begun to doubt whether you were still there after all. They were panicked that there may have been a lapse in security and you had left without them noticing."

Karl responded gruffly. "Remember who you are speaking to Baxter. I am at the house. I left my phone in one of the rooms and only just realised I had left it. I came in and found the battery depleted and upon charging found you and Sebastian had been trying to contact me."

"Sebastian is on a private plane back to the UK as we speak, you will have difficulty speaking to him directly. Karl, you do not understand. The company network may have been breached."

Karl sat down heavily on the bed. "What do you mean?" Baxter briefly outlined his discussions with Sebastian. Rotschlossen knew more than Baxter about the situation at hand. It was that street whore's brother. He worked for the Company, it would be him that had used it against their systems.

"Sebastian said that if I was able to contact you then I should warn you that the Company might be making a move against us."

"Did he ask you to tell me anything else?"

"No that was all he said. What does he mean the company is moving against us? Are you expecting the company to fold?" Baxter's voice was panicked by the notion of this.

"Do not be ridiculous Baxter you fool. Our company is going nowhere. If you speak to Sebastian before I do, tell him I shall meet him at the office as soon as possible." Rotschlossen cut off the phone call with a jab of his thumb. If the boy from the Company was accessing the database and trying to find information then he may be on his way here. He may be here already.

Karl looked at the open bedroom door and broke in to a run back downstairs to the basement. He stopped momentarily in the hall to collect a Heckler and Koch MP5 from a cupboard, loading it with a fresh magazine, before rushing back down the stairs.

Chapter 60

Steph worked the restraints open to free Annabel. She moved to the side of the bed and tried to stand but collapsed almost immediately from her own weight. Her feet had no sense of feeling due to the tightness of the belts holding her in place on the bed. They began to tingle and then burn with pain as the blood slowly found it's way back to her extremities. The plaster on the back of her hand itched and she tore it off in disgust. She looked at Steph and collapsed in to his arms with relief. "Thank you Steph. Thank you, thank you, thank you." She cried her thanks over and over as he rubbed her back, trying to comfort and hush her. "Did you see what he did to those girls. Did you see?" Her eyes were wide with fear and a need to know somebody other than her had witnessed at least something of the atrocities on the screen.

"Yes. I saw." His voice was emotionless. Steph felt as if his entire world had been ripped from under him.

"Jamie?" He nodded in acknowledgement. "I'm sorry Steph." She whispered.

"It's not your fault Annabel. How did you get here? Did Sebastian bring you?"

"No Sebastian had to go away suddenly on business." She quickly explained what had happened up to the point where he found her. "Thank you for saving me Steph."

"You're not saved yet, we need to get moving, Rotschlossen will be back soon."

Chapter 61

As if on cue gunfire rained down on Steph, raking across his arm and back. He fell forwards with shock, Annabel screamed and her already wavering balance was lost, crashing heavily behind the bed.

A shout came from the now open chamber door. "He is dead now Miss Annabel, nobody to save you." In response steady gunfire was returned at Rotschlossen, he saw the movement just in time and dived back through the door, the bullets removing large chunks of the thickened glass of the windows. Rotschlossen looked at them both wildly, Steph now standing, a look of realization coming to his face. *The body suit.* He pushed the button to close the door and activated the gas again before running off back up the stairs, he turned to the left and headed to the concealed armoury. *The Company must have given him that suit, he would not have been able to procure it otherwise.* Karl was sure of that, however if that was the case then that meant this attack on him was sanctioned. What he had thought to be just one agent with a vendetta may have the backing of the whole Company. With Sebastian's help he would bring them to their knees for this treachery. The suit was of a special polymer made by the special project R and D section of their company, it was resistant to bullet fire, even at close range. Only 5 had been made and one of these had been sold to the company earlier in the year for them to test. The rest were held in a secure location. *Every disease has it's cure.* Karl wrenched open a drawer and entered a special code, scanned his fingerprint and retina's, before giving his vocal password. A section of the wall slid open revealing a room of weapons, body armour and other useful accoutrements.
Unfortunately, not one of those suits. He did however have the next best thing. From a shelf he snatched some fresh magazines, ejecting the one already in the MP5 and loading one of them. The others he stuffed in to pockets and his belt. He turned and with a wave closed the door.

Chapter 62

As Rotschlossen ran back towards the stairs Steph ran for the door. It was the only way out. He had made a terrible mistake, he should never have ventured in to the chamber before killing Rotschlossen. *Stupid, stupid, stupid.* The door was sealed tightly shut but worse he detected a slightly sweet smell in the air. Some sort of gas was being released, he was already feeling a little groggy. At the door he fired some more shots at the dent he had already made in the glass. A small hole about an inch across was made but although not designed to be bullet proof the glass was still very resilient. Steph clamped his mouth over the hole and took a deep breath of the clean air from the control room. "Annabel, quickly come here." She stumbled across the room towards him. "Put your mouth on here and breathe, quickly." She did as he asked and her glazed eyes cleared a little. Steph took a turn breathing again and gestured she should do the same. "Take in as much air as you can and hold it. Go over to that corner behind that table, put your hands over your ears and wait there." Annabel drew a big breath and half ran, half fell to where he had indicated. He took deep breaths through the hole and then filled it with some plastic explosive from his pack. Carefully inserting the detonators, he then ran back to Annabel, barely behind the table when he pushed the remote.

The wave of the explosion and sound in the confined room was excruciating, shards of glass from the window flew inwards as well as out in to the control room. The table offered a good level of protection but Annabel cried out as a thin shard left a cut across her arm. Steph checked it quickly, it wasn't deep. He tore off some of her top and quickly bandaged it. At the same time pulling her up and dashing towards the door. They had to get out before Rotschlossen got back otherwise they would be trapped. The door was well made, he had deliberately used a sizeable amount of explosive but the door itself was relatively unaffected, only the glass window was shattered, and even that not fully. The control room however was a mess. He helped Annabel through, careful not to slice her bare feet to ribbons on the broken glass. Steph carried her over most of it and then pushed in front of her as they got to the stairs. *Rotschlossen must have heard the explosion.* As he reached the top of the stairs he saw Rotschlossen had more than heard the explosion. It must have vibrated up through the house and some of the basement had collapsed on top of him. He reached over to check his pulse, it was weak but unfortunately it was still there. He considered putting a bullet in to his face right now but remembered his vow. Rotschlossen was not to have a nice easy death, he was going to pay for what he did to Jamie.

"Is he dead?"

"No." Steph pulled some cable ties from his pack and flipped Karl's limp body over, pulling his arms tight behind him. Annabel was distracting him, it felt wrong to have her watch him, it was as if it was Jamie. He could not do this with her here. "He will be but I can't do it with you here."

"Why? I want to watch him die." Tears of anger were flowing from the corner of Annabel's eyes. Steph walked over to her and spoke gently.

"You think you do but trust me you don't." He had to get her out. "Come on let's go."

"What about him?"

"I'll be back for *that* once you are out of this house."

They walked back up to the ground floor and followed the maze of corridors back to the main front door. There had been no guards in the vicinity of the house, Annabel would have to follow the drive until she ran in to a patrol. They knew she was meant to be here, she would be safe there while he finished Rotschlossen. Steph was relieved to find that opening the door from the inside was substantially easier than from the outside. He opened the door and pushed Annabel out in to the cold night air. "Follow the driveway until you meet a guard patrol. I'll be right behind you." She stumbled away down the driveway and he closed the door.

As the door closed a small LED at the side changed from green to red and a soft click came from the door. *Rotschlossen.* He tried the door again but knew it would be futile. It was locked. *So that's how you want it.* For the second time that night Steph's hunt for Rotschlossen was on. This time with one critical difference.

Rotschlossen was hunting him too.

Chapter 63

Annabel stumbled down the driveway. The smooth gravel reminded her of a beach she went to as a small child. She could see the sun shining, her Mum and Dad laughing. Times were good then. She could see the vast sea. She had chased the waves as they went out and ran back screaming and laughing as they chased her back ashore. *Screams.* Not like the screams of all those girls. Annabel realised someone was shouting at her, a man with a gun pointed in her face, a bright torch mounted underneath was very bright she thought. It was hurting her eyes. She could not seem to focus on what he was saying. "Sebastian." She called out for him as everything swamped her and she fell.

She felt the strong arms of the men with guns catch her. They were carrying her somewhere but she did not care. Rotschlossen did not have her anymore. It felt as if she was floating away. She lost consciousness wondering why the men were shouting.

Chapter 64

Steph took careful steps to immediately melt in to the shadows. The little alcoves would serve him well except he did not know this place as remotely well as Rotschlossen did. He knew little about Rotschlossen's training too. He was Sebastian's assistant but it was rumoured he was also his bodyguard and had been since Sebastian was a child but he was older now. Older meant slower but it also meant more experienced. He retraced his steps back to the basement entrance, he saw that the door was still slightly ajar as he and Annabel had left it. He remembered seeing at least two other ways to get in and out of the basement when he was searching, Rotschlossen could have used either of those and they were just the ones he knew about. He decided to go in to the basement and track him from where he had last seen him, hoping he was not waiting to ambush him. Steph took the old stairs slowly, although well maintained they were old and made of wood, prone to creak, likely to give him away. He reached the bottom of the stairs and quickly crossed the basement to where Rotschlossen had been unconscious. Steph knew he would be gone but it was the tracks he was looking for, not the person. He could see from the dust where Rotschlossen had managed to get to his feet and cross the room. Checking the shadows as he went, he crossed to the wall where the trail led. There was some blood on a nail and on the floor beneath that the cable tie he had used to bind Rotschlossen. He cursed himself, knowing he should have bound his legs too and done a better job on his hands. There were small spots of blood on the floor leading to one of the other exits, Steph followed it to the stairs, these were stone, much easier to climb without giving himself away. That would be why Karl had chosen them.

Once again he surfaced from the basement in to one of the many corridors. The night although cold, was clear and this corridor was bathed in the soft white glow of the moon. He could see a dirty handprint on the door in the corner of the corridor. Slowly he approached it, he checked his gun and slowly eased the handle around. The door made a soft click which seemed to echo down the corridors and point accusingly at Steph's presence. He held his breath and waited, then, when nothing happened, he slowly eased open the door, letting it swing open on it's own momentum so he could cover the room with his gun. The room turned out to be a stairwell. Gun first he advanced up the stairs, his body taut, ready for whatever he should encounter. He made a mental note to try and put his body or arms in the way of any shots as the suit would protect those areas but not his head. Steph followed the trail to the top floor. He came on to another corridor. The impeccably kept house made tracking Rotschlossen surprisingly easy. The dirt from the small collapse in the basement stood in striking contrast to the highly polished floors and carefully cleaned carpets. He proceeded halfway down the corridor and the trail stopped in front of some double doors. Rotschlossen must be inside. Steph tried to decide what to do. He doubted Rotschlossen would be drawn out but equally going in could be suicide. He carefully weighed up his options.

"Come in Mr. Thebe." Rotschlossen's voice called from behind the doors. "Unless you intend to stand outside all night?" Steph looked up to the PIR sensors in the corner of the corridors and the small camera's mounted beside them. He might as well have stomped straight here without a care in the world. Rotschlossen had been monitoring him the entire time anyway. He decided to enter the room fast, roll in the opposite direction and try to get the upper hand on him. Checking the suit was in place and praying he did not get shot in the head, Steph slowly eased one of the doors open, looking in to the room as he went. When the door was open about a foot he charged in to the room, before spinning back in the opposite direction, eyes darting around to look for cover. He felt his hopes collapse as he saw there was no cover. The room was empty except for Rotschlossen.

A single shot was fired and Steph cried out in a yell mid-roll as the bullet tore through his shoulder. The shock hit him immediately, not so much at being shot but that the suit had not offered any protection. It had resisted a barrage of bullets earlier.

"You seem surprised Mr Thebe." Rotschlossen flicked a single bullet towards him which Steph caught with his good arm, it had a strange rainbow sheen that caused his fingers to glide, almost as if they were repelled, from the coating. Whatever it was, it clearly cut through the suit as if it wasn't there. "Where do you think the suit came from?" Rotschlossen raised a weary eyebrow. He levelled the gun at Steph almost apologetically. "You must die of course."

"WAIT!" Steph held out his hand. "First tell me. Why her? Why Jamie?"

"You mean to say you have not worked it out yet? I feel less sorry about killing you now. MacLeavey had always said you were so intelligent, so skilled." He leaned closer as if confiding a great secret. "She was a homeless whore." Karl smiled as Steph's face tightened. "She was taken because nobody would miss her, nobody cared."

"I cared."

"Really? Is that why you abandoned her to join the Company? Do you even know what your stepfather Todd did too Jamie once you left?" Steph glared up at him. Todd and his mother had been killed in a car accident shortly after Jamie had run away. He hadn't been responsible for the crash but he wished he was. "When your mother went out, or when he could get time alone with Jamie, he used to touch her. He used to touch her and tell her that she was dirty and had no choice, that her big brother was not there to protect her any more." Steph reached for the gun that had flown from his grip when he had been shot. Karl released another round in to his leg. Steph contained the scream but stayed where he was. "You see they were all taken because none of them would be missed. Young girls are homeless for a reason but normally the ultimate reason is that the people closest to them either stopped caring or stopped existing. By the time they were taken all of them were desperate for some comfort and that is what they received, at first." A sinister look flitted across his face. "You would be astounded to learn what a girl will do to try and save her own life, even more astounded to find out what they would do to have you end it." He sighed again and raised the gun. "I am sorry Mr Thebe but our time has expired. It is quite the mess you and the Company have started here and I think some lessons will have to be taught. Good bye."

Steph glared in to his eyes. "Fuck you."

Chapter 65

Annabel opened her eyes as the soft voice whispered her name, calling her awake. "SEBASTIAN!" She leapt from the cot she had been laid upon and wrapped her arms around him. She started to cry heavily in to his shoulder as he made comforting noises and stroked her hair.

"Annabel. Where is Karl."

"Hopefully he's dead!" She had a look of venom as she spat the words.

"Annabel that is quite rude, Karl has been my friend since I was born, it is important that I speak to him."

"Perhaps you should be more careful about the company you keep then!" He looked to the guard behind him but he shrugged and shook his head. "*Karl* is in the house with Steph. Steph is going to kill him!" She said the words triumphantly.

"Why would Steph want to kill Karl?"

"Because Karl killed Jamie." She turned her eyes away from his and whispered. "Karl killed a lot of people." She looked up to the house just in time to see one of the wings explode. The shockwave shook the guard house and sent guards from all over running towards the house, Sebastian at the lead. Sirens were already sounding in the distance and flashing lights could be seen approaching the entry to the only road. All they could do was stand helplessly and wait.

Chapter 66

Annabel walked doggedly towards the lobby of the police station. The police had made a rudimentary search of the house but had been quick to close the case based on Annabel's statement and she thought probably some higher influence. It was clear Sebastian had no knowledge of the situation as he was in a different country when it transpired, also as Karl was so trusted he was pretty much given free reign to spend and build as he felt was necessary, so they had released him very quickly. She was not entirely sure who Steph had worked for or what connections Sebastian had but it was clear the police officers were uneasy about all of this and were quick to get the matter resolved. The strangest thing was the television. Between her interviews she had taken a break in a room with a television. While she drank her coffee she had flicked through the channels until she found the news. There was no mention of the explosion, no mention of Karl or Steph's deaths. No mention of the murder of all those girls. *Perhaps it was too early.* She had thought. When the police told her she was free to go Annabel breathed a sigh of relief. Her head and arm ached, the bandage itched. The police officer who had been interviewing her asked if she would like a lift anywhere, the relief turned to dread as she realised there was nowhere for them to take her. She sullenly shook her head and stood to leave. The silly hopes she had held for a future with Sebastian seemed so distant now. He would blame her for what happened to Karl, he would wish he had never tried to help her. He had come and gone in just a few short days. The tears ran silently down her cheeks. The thought of returning to the streets dowsed the last flicker of her resolve as effectively as death itself. She wondered if she would be better off dead. She chastised herself, knowing with everything that had happened in the last 24 hours she most certainly did not want to be dead. Her thoughts drifted to Jamie, Christine and Steph. She walked through the doors to the lobby and was somewhat taken aback to see Sebastian sitting on one of the uncomfortable, red, leather chairs.

Sebastian rose as she walked towards him. "You waited?"

"But of course." He smiled good-naturedly.

"I thought you would blame me."

"I am afraid we are all responsible for our own actions Annabel."

She felt the slight spark of hope begin to rekindle inside.

A limousine was waiting for them outside. It drove them to the penthouse building and they sat in silence. They rode the elevator to the top floor and stepped inside. Annabel felt shell shocked.

"I'm exhausted."

Sebastian smiled. "I am also. I have flown to New York and back in the past twenty four hours and have had only a few hours sleep." Finally now it was truly over. Karl was dead, he could not hurt her or anyone else anymore. Perhaps the future she had dared to dream of could become a reality. Annabel embraced the warmth of the apartment, so different to the cold of the streets she had feared returning to just moments before. She closed her eyes and took a deep breath, turning to Sebastian and looking at him with her big, deep eyes. "I still can hardly believe this has all happened." Sebastian looked deep in to her eyes, his gaze firmly on her own. The subtle flashes and movements that hid within the depths of his eyes had now come to forefront. What Annabel saw there now caused a trickle of uncertainty run up her spine. A nagging doubt crept through her bones, chilling her completely despite the warmth of the room. As Sebastian turned and pushed a button to secure the locks on the door, recognition flashed in to her mind. The way he moved. The man on the video he had moved the same way but it had been Karl, it must have been Karl, she knew it was. Terror froze her to the spot, constricting her throat, she stood staring helplessly as Sebastian turned his attention back to her. "Annabel, sometimes, even if you do not want to believe something, in your heart you know it's true."